AMERICAN COPPER

AMERICAN COPPER

Shann Ray

UNBRIDLED BOOKS

Unbridled Books

Copyright © 2015 by Shann Ray

Library of Congress Cataloging-in-Publication Data

Ray, Shann.
American copper / Shann Ray.
pages ; cm
ISBN 978-1-60953-121-8
I. Title.
PS3618.A9828A84 2015
813'.6--dc23
2015011741

1 3 5 7 9 10 8 6 4 2

Book Design by SH • CV

First Printing

for Jennifer

I am afraid to own a Body—
I am afraid to own a Soul—

EMILY DICKINSON

AMERICAN COPPER

I.

=✦=

The train moves west, tight-bound in an upward

arc along the sidewall of tremendous mountains,

the movement of metal and muscle working above

the tree line, chugging out black smoke. Smoke, black

first against the grayish rock, the granite face of the

mountain, then higher and farther back black into

the keen blue of sky without clouds.

=✦=

EVELYNNE LOWRY, 1907

I.

DAILY, MEN descended into the earth, going where no man belonged, taking more than men deserved, their faces wracked with indifference, their hands dirtied with soot from the depths of the mountain.

Aboveground, the last lights of evening shimmered before darkness fell.

She held her father's hand as they walked in the upper meadow beyond the ranch house, the place from which she saw sky and moon and stars, and below her far off in the top floor, the flicker of lantern glow from her father's window. Five years old and slight, face chalk white framed by dark auburn hair, her eyes were the green of glacial pools, slate green and gray, the iris encircled in black. Her fingers were cold. Full of fright her father called her. Afraid of people mainly, he thought, and specifically men.

In the meadow when he pointed, her eyes followed his arm to

the sky. "Cygnus the Swan. Vega. Altair. Albireo. The Summer Triangle. Daughter, do you see?" She saw stars more white than silver in the outer dark. She made out the triangle and, within the triangle, lights cold and still as if held in place like a basket of bright stones.

"Tomorrow night, you recite for my guests," he said. "Don't disappoint me." In his voice a hint of the old immigrant accent.

She was the child of her father. "Yes, Papa," she said. As he drew her close and touched her face a night bird called from the forest.

THE NEXT MORNING he took her with him along the shallow cut banks of the river. The sun low on its rise to the zenith, he went to one knee, hushing her as he held her shoulders and pointed a few feet ahead. *"Lycaena phlaeas americana,"* he said.

Flickering like minuscule fires, light-winged butterflies mingled among the timothy over the water. "What do the words mean?" she asked.

More harshly than he intended, he said, "Quiet."

The sun shimmered, aslant at the river's bend.

"American Copper," he whispered.

Larksong. The percussion of a mountain jay.

When he touched her hair there was a tenderness he knew to be the God in him. He cherished her. She let her head meet his hand.

The butterfly brood vivid below them.

"Even now," he said under his breath, "copper in the air."

Her hair too has copper, he thought, the sun on the curve behind her ear, the glint of her hair nearly bronze among the sheen of black. She is so like her mother. He let his thoughts linger.

"Is there more, Papa?" she inquired.

"Yes, Evelynne," he said. She bore her mother's name. "Butterflies of the Lycaenids, or gossamer-winged family," he continued softly, "of the race *L. phlaeas americana*, binomial name *Lycaena phlaeas* derived from the Greek *phlego*, 'to burn up.' Named by Carl Linnaeus of Sweden in 1761. Of the kingdom Animalia, phylum Anthropoda, class Insecta, order Lepidoptera. In Montana not simply the Small Copper or the Common Copper but the American Copper butterfly."

She smiled openly, pressing her torso back into his chest. She placed her hands over his. Exhaling, he took in the river and its environs.

"They are so shiny, Papa," she said, "like candles with black fringe and black spots."

He chuckled while she grew silent. A single butterfly moved toward her as if climbing poorly made stairs. The creature came close before lighting on her forearm. Evelynne's body seemed to unfold outward. The wings closed and hinged open again. Her hair felt touched with electricity.

"Still," he whispered, but he needn't have, he thought.

Her fortitude, he knew, was like the mountain.

2.

SLENDER AS A sapling, she stood that night on a black hickory table in the great room. Her father was a man hard as granite with other men, a man of fist, commerce, and copper. Josef, he called himself. Others called him the Baron. Josef Lowry had more money than the Montana State Treasury. Born in America but Czech by blood, he had changed his surname, Vavrik, to the English equivalent, Lowry, and made men suffer. He was un-friendly with Washington but respected. His men dug copper from the ground. He sent it by train to the centers of industry.

I move this country, he thought.

He smiled for her. For her brother too, but Tomás was in town with the tutor Josef retained to prepare him for Harvard, where he would make his father proud.

Tonight the dignitaries of Montana gathered with their wives in the great room, wide-eyed. The men endured with slick hair, part lines clean and straight, faces shaven, black or brown full beaver felt hats in hand, derbies and straights, tapers and cowboy hats. The women wore gloves and fine dresses, beads like gemstones set in silk at shoulder or hip. People milled beneath the electric burn of a Bohemian crystal chandelier shipped from Prague, a many-armed work of art—high, wide, full of light, the room lit to every corner. Alder, pine, and maple at floor and ceiling. Great ponderosa logs stripped of their bark for walls. The tart smell of fresh wood. Throughout, deer and antelope antlers were set in European mounts, clean skull with darkened horns, the death's-heads like silent touchstones of days he'd ridden out at dawn, returning with the animal lain across the rump of his horse. A comfort to him. A sense of solace. He watched the women, their flowing curls and well-shaped gowns a reminder of the wife he'd lost. His face started to crack, but he steeled himself before he called to his daughter in a loud voice.

"Evelynne, child of my heart."

She smiled. Blushed.

Too meek, he thought. He went to her at the table and stood before her, holding her hand. He beamed at the people and they applauded even before she began. If only his father were here, he thought, a man he imagined dead of poverty or anguish. They hadn't spoken since St. Louis. He'd hold his father's head in his low convalescent bed, mine worker, railroad hand, track layer, fighter crushed by rock. In Josef's waking dream the old man rose and stood tall, smiling like Josef had never seen. The Governor and his lieutenants, the head of the railway and his henchmen, they were all here now in the public dining room with their women to listen to Josef's daughter because Josef wanted them to be here and because they knew he was richer and more powerful than the lot of them.

Dark wine in tall glasses. Prime cuts of Montana beefsteak. Tumblers of cognac. Thick cigars. The air perfumed by feminine skin, they dined like royalty as they held their women. The men guffawed and bragged as they tried to pump themselves up in the face of their host's wealth, his mountain castle so unlike the paper shacks and hillside dugouts he'd known as a boy. Tonight, he thought, his princess was like a small queen, with her crushed-velvet dress and white lace collar, white silk gloves, and her mother's pearl necklace, the gift of oysters of the Orient tripled around her delicate neck. His face wanted to break again. His wife should be here.

He set his voice like a rail before him.

"I present to you the Queen of Montana!"

He flourished his hand as everyone applauded, hooted, hollered.

Evelynne's face flushed.

Josef made eye contact, nodded, the aftertaste of buttered steak in his mouth. She lifted her eyes, then proceeded to recite without error ten Shakespearean sonnets, each made with fourteen knotted lines filled with tongue twists and turns, three quatrains and a couplet, one hundred forty lines in all. She delivered with gusto and fire: "Shall I compare thee to a summer's day? Thou art more lovely and more temperate, … And summer's lease hath all too short a date: Sometime too hot the eye of heaven shines." She raised her hands in a V. "Yet in these thoughts myself almost despising, haply I think on thee, and then my state, like to the lark at break of day arising from sullen earth, sings hymns at heaven's gate." The women and the men stood, their eyes alive to her performance. "Love alters not with his brief hours and weeks, but bears it out even to the edge of doom." She punched a fist to her chest. They gasped. A few men chortled uncomfortably but were hushed by those near. "My love is as a fever, longing still for that which longer nurseth the disease, feeding on that which doth preserve the ill, th' uncertain sickly appetite to please. … For I have sworn thee fair, and thought thee bright, who art as black as hell, as dark as night."

Josef was seen mouthing the words. He thought of his father's thick accent. The King's English was the English his children knew. Shakespeare the pinnacle.

When she finished, the people roared their approval. Josef lifted Evelynne from the table and set her on the hardwood floor. She looked at the bodies flowing toward her. She turned to her father and tucked herself to his pant legs, but he bellowed with laughter. She pinched his leg before she ran wildly from the room, his voice booming behind her.

"Well done, Evelynne! Well done!" and quieter, "Come back, child."

But she stayed away.

When the people left he watched from the door as they walked across the wood of the veranda before receding into the darkness. They made their way mostly to carriages and one or two automobiles. He looked up once and saw the encompassing sky, numberless with stars. But he turned his face down before the beauty could unravel him. Back inside, he found her trembling beneath her bed. He pulled her out by her heel. Holding her to his chest, he lay down with her on the small bed. Touched the palm of his hand, chill, to her warm face. *"Kuráž,"* he whispered over her. "Courage," and soon she slept.

Josef's father had been little respected. Josef and his brother, Leopold, the first generation born in this country, his father had raised them Czech while paying for some small English education. What he knew they'd need for this land. By trade a laborer, he was despised by many. In St. Louis, the last civilized place before the great expanse, he'd taught both sons to give no quarter.

Josef wiped his eyes with the heel of his hand, rose and went to his liquor cabinet and tipped back whiskey until his chest was hot.

He strode through the house, a hunger in him to break the world.

There had been a wildness to his coming west, but now he was numb. He missed his wife terribly. Her worry drove her, her fear of wilderness and wild things, bear, badger, wolf, even Indians. He'd taken her to powwows so she'd see how being subjugated had largely taken their will. The Blackfeet, big and fearsome during the Indian Wars, quiet now in the high northwest corner of Montana on the windswept steppe below the great mountains. The Crow in the far southeast, enemies of the Cheyenne whose lands abutted theirs but lay still farther east and whose society of leadership involved a council of forty-four chiefs Josef thought to be a modern miracle. Four above forty. He'd kept a Cheyenne hand once who'd spoken of the council. Paid the Indian even less than he paid the Chinese, though the hand was uncanny with horses.

Too many voices, Josef thought. Yet they abide, even thrive.

The hand had said the chiefs served not themselves but the

people. As for himself, Josef couldn't countenance subservience.

In America, there was resource and power, power under-ground and power over, the will to extract metal from rock, to separate flesh from bone. He would be positioned above other men. He would exhaust the storehouses of God. He'd be a king in this land, he thought. He felt sorry for himself. He didn't want to drink, but he propped himself on his elbow, drinking bourbon from the bottle until he heard the glass butt of it thud on the floor below him. He fell asleep in a stupor, his head tilted over the side of the bed.

In the morning he approached the mirror in his bathroom. His eyes were red and blown out. He struck himself flat-handed in the face. He struck himself again, watching the pink of his skin bloom and spread. His look began to darken. His pupils turned to points of black lead among fields of water. He slapped him-self in the face for near a quarter hour. By the end of it his hair was wrung out over his forehead, and his neck glistened with sweat. He needed more wealth, he thought.

He washed his face in the hand basin before he dressed and went out into the great room.

3.

EVELYNNE HAD CALLED her brother Babo since she first spoke. To her, Tomás was joy, protection, and peace. Even when the house seemed to collapse under her father's drunkenness, the sorrow took a different shape because of Tomás. Always at night, a silence fell. The lights darkened, then the oil lamps went out. Then came the startle of something heavy thrown to the floor, the sound of breaking glass and Josef's boot steps in the halls, a maniacal cadence over which he shouted invectives that as a child made her flee to the standing closet, a large black oak wardrobe with thick doors she'd enter and quickly close. As she crouched inside, her body shook and she cried. When the doors opened she feared her father's ruined face. But most often it was Tomás who came to her. He was already a man then, more slender than his father, taller, wider in the chest, but he'd crawl into the wardrobe and tuck her head into the crook of his neck and rest his hands on her arms until she calmed. He held her and spoke words that made her heart hurt, "You are beloved in this house, Eve. Don't worry. He misses our mother. All will be well."

But the memory of her father killing the Chinese stable boy Liu over a single horsing incident infected her mind. Her brother's presence had a curative effect. Like her, he had seen their father's outburst. She wondered where he placed the knowledge. In the morning, he'd walk into her room playing light harmonica. Old hillbilly songs on the mouth organ ... "Who's Gonna Shoe Your Pretty Little Feet," and "Cacklin' Hen Blues." A quickstep on "Huskin' Bee." The southern wail for "Chased Old Satan Through the Door." "Keep on!" she'd tell him, clapping, and he'd start in again.

It was also in those early years that Evelynne witnessed her father severely harm Tomás on three occasions. Just after Christmas of Tomás's thirteenth year he suffered two broken ribs when Josef hit him in the side with the butt of an axe. She let out a scream, but Tomás didn't utter a sound. Later the same year, when Josef bent his son's hand backward in a burst of anger at the kitchen table, breaking his wrist, Tomás yelled as he fell to the floor. He clutched his hand to his chest and sobbed. She went to him, even tried to kiss his face, but he wouldn't be comforted. Not two years later Tomás sustained a broken leg when his father caught him sleeping in the field and ran him over with a loaded oxcart. The family doctor repaired the young man each time as if a day's work was nothing but violence.

Yet the spirit of Tomás remained to Evelynne indomitable. She found him in the trees sometimes, singing deep, abiding songs. He makes music, she told herself. He is a singer.

At the ranch, to teach her to ride, he secured from her father

her first real horse, a chestnut filly she named Chloe, honey-sweet and fast in the leg, raised from a foal. The riding too was a blessing to her. He helped her train the horse and taught her horsemanship, taking her with him until she understood. "Watch the eyes and ears, the tail," he said. "Recognize the posture first, Eve. Is the horse calm or afraid? Is the outline of the horse relaxed or high and arched, showing alarm? When you gain his trust, you can settle even a spooked horse. The ears point in the direction of the horse's attention. Both ears forward is elegant, but when riding, the horse needs to have at least one ear on you. If a horse pins her ears back she's angry or afraid. If she moves them back and forth, she's confused or uncertain. When the ears go flat a kick is coming."

He put his hand on Chloe's forehead. "Watch her when we teach her anything new. Her mouth is tight. Then when she gets it, her mouth relaxes and she chews. When she wants to bite, she opens her mouth and bares her teeth. When she just barely opens her mouth and cranes her neck, she likes the groom you're giving. This means you've got her just right."

Evelynne grew up in his stride. She saw that he handled men and horses with dignity. She hoped to emulate him. Certainly he and their father shared a bitter disregard for one another's ways, but Tomás did not buck his father, choosing rather the road of obedience under the browbeating and hard labor it was to be Josef Lowry's son. Even Tomás's deference Evelynne recognized as an attempt to shield her from their father. For her part, she thought Tomás would be better off trying to break their father's will, not bow to it, but it wasn't her place to say. Besides, the men of her father's operation flocked to Tomás. They worked like madmen under his direction. Regardless, Tomás was evidence to her: God made brothers for their sisters, to walk together in this life.

His loyalty raised her up.

Chan Wu too was a bulwark, her father's elderly manservant a presence steady and unceasing even when her own moods rose or fell.

Still, her brother's leaving for college and war was an amputation.

AT SEVENTEEN SHE came into her body fully formed, her spirit no longer meek but striking, and others saw that she was made more of avalanche or forest fire than bushels of wheat or the quiet night. Her face lively, she loved the light. Her hair black and auburn and straight to her waist, she became difficult for men to forget.

But it would be long before Evelynne entered society. The land was home, the cant of sun that crested the mountains to the east and spread upward over the budding city, place of bustle and production, the sun at dawn on a stepwise progression until it reached her father's city house. For now her father had her living not out on the ranch but in the Chicago-style three-story Victorian in Butte, with hardwood interior made of squared-off pillars and wainscoted wood, crown molding that lined ceilings, and decorative baseboards that fortified the edges of each floor. Everywhere the smell of lacquer, the level texture of fine silver, five ground-floor rooms with twelve-foot beveled mirrors. Large framed windows of leaded glass graced the house into which the light seeped and finally flared as the day arched over the mountain.

She walked through the front room to the dark wood mantle over the fireplace where a blue-toned photograph of her mother was set in a gilded frame. Evelynne was more naturally drawn away from the industry of the city to the wilderness where she could be alone in great tracts of land, inviolable and fierce of their own accord. She lifted the frame, pressing the photograph to her chest before she set it back and went outside to the carriage house. She rode Chloe down Main Street before leading her into the wooded mountains all the way to the upper reach of the gorge along the westward passage. The outlay of the river was far below. The cut of mountains to the riverbed. She arrived shortly at the narrows of the canyon where bears in twos and threes worked near the river's mouth. The high heat of summer's decline. She kept to the ridge above while below, the bears lumbered from a thin sandbar into the water. They nearly butted shoulders as they took paw swipes at the stepped riffles and threw fish onto the banks.

They ate like kings.

When she dismounted, she walked through the high timothy to the bole of an aspen. Here a swath of trees led down the mountain through the rock to the water. She thought of her brother's grace. She sat down, her back to the tree as she watched the bears. They moved like great brown dogs back and forth between the water and the land.

When a ruckus of voices came up from halfway down the mountain, she rose and stepped beside Chloe, holding the horse's neck as she leaned out. In the trees below, she made out a group of five men from the mines. Young, and young at heart, they laughed and spoke loudly. They walked in boots near worn to the bone, their canvas clothes dark from mine work, their hands and faces near blackened. On the spit farther down, the bears paid them no heed. For their part, the men did not recognize the beasts' proximity. Light of foot and sturdy, the way they cavorted and carried on made Evelynne smile. She decided to follow them. She did not want to be seen. She clicked her tongue. Chloe came along behind.

Farther west with the entire canyon laid out ahead, the men descended to a lip of rock high over a bend in the river where the water pooled into a large bowl before it spilled west through a crease at the base of the mountains. She stayed hidden as the young men disrobed until they were naked but for a cotton gonch.

All but the bearded one gingerly approached the edge and looked over. Eve was mesmerized as one by one they leapt from the lip of the rock.

Their high screams of joy and abandon echoed in the basin. Their bodies struck the water, disappearing before they emerged again far downriver.

The bearded one stayed back until they all hung in the flow downstream where the river grew still, and he called to them. "Hey, you yella-bellies!" he shouted, then gave a horse laugh that rang from the canyon walls. He took a number of paces into the forest before he turned, ran to the edge and launched himself headfirst into the void. Evelynne caught her breath. His arms reached out like the wings of a swan. He angled himself, arcing downward, singular and of a symmetry she had never seen.

His body pierced the water like an arrow.

The men yelled, clapping as they called out to him, and when he came to where they waded near shore they lifted him from the water. They slapped his chest and shoulders and spoke his name. "Abram, ah Abram! Bravo, Abram!"

From her vantage point in the trees, the horse behind her shoulder, she watched them. In the afternoon sun their bodies shone as if made of white marble. An upswell of emotion entered her chest. Tears came to her eyes. Why? she thought. She wanted neither company nor companionship, but she found it beautiful how they pulled one another from the current and slapped each other's backs. They were as supple as lions. She wanted to stretch out her hands and touch them.

With difficulty they made their way up the rock face until they crested the lip again. They put on their clothes, then walked into the woods on a line toward town.

When the heat was still high and the men gone, Evelynne walked down the mountainside with Chloe to the rock ledge. No wind. Birdsong from far off. She removed her boots and stockings, her blouse, long skirt, and riding breeches. She stood in the singlet of her undergarment, thin cotton to the neck, elbow, and knee. She positioned Chloe sideways at the rock lip. She rubbed the horse's coat at the shoulders and rump, ran her hands over the jaw, and looked into the animal's eyes as Chloe's lips parted slightly. Evelynne climbed into the saddle, then climbed awkwardly farther up until she stood atop her horse. The sun was hot on her arms.

Chloe shook her mane but otherwise kept still. Evelynne

wouldn't dive, she wasn't foolhardy. The river was far below. Fear flushed her neck.

She swallowed once, looked across the gorge, and leapt.

The ground fell away as she flew downward. The drop was ungodly and the water seemed to rush toward her but the earth was awash in light, the water silver and transparent below, as if she had leapt into heaven only to descend to a deeper, clearer heaven from which no one could displace her, in which no one could be displaced. She plummeted into the water where she was taken by the current's power, swept abruptly downstream in a swift arc. At last her limbs came right again and she sensed light borne from above as she swam for the surface and broke through. She drew air into her lungs as if for the first time, then let herself breathe as her body floated farther downriver.

Finally she cut broad strokes to the shore. When she found her footing and emerged from the river, she was breathless. Gathering herself she shouted with all her might, her voice echoing off the canyon walls. She waited for the silence, then lay down on her back. Small, smooth stones pressed against her shoulder blades. She put her hands behind her head and sighed. At the height of the rock face, high overhead, Chloe moved at her leisure, pulling grass.

When evelynne arrived in Butte, it was dusk. She patted Chloe down and had her stabled before she entered the house and strode past her father where he was seated at his desk in the war room.

"Where have you been, child?" he said.

"About," she answered but continued walking the long hall, then up the stairs to her bedroom, where she was compelled to capture her thoughts on paper before they eluded her. She wrote by lamplight deep into the dark, her father bringing her jerked venison, cheese, and black tea past midnight.

HAVING DELIVERED THE food, her father touched her shoulder and returned to his bed. She'd be famished, he thought, when the work came on her this way. He turned his pillow over, folding his hands on his chest. He watched the stars out his bedroom window. Keep her soul, he thought. Keep her. Evelynne was the one delicate creature left in his life, and he would protect her above all. Man of copper, man of brick and mortar, and man of this house, the Baron touched the wall over his head. He admired the house, interior of walnut, mahogany, and hickory, a house over all other houses in the city, featuring a large vaulted library he'd filled floor to ceiling for her. History, government, geology, poetry, a ladder on wheel and track. The child had devoted herself to the room, a place in which his love was on occasion spoken.

He loved her poems. Tutored, nannied, dressed in fine clothes, and set alone among the wilderness, she was cultured but as yet not wholly refined. He breathed in deeply and exhaled. She had come home this day after hours away, her hair disheveled, her clothes smelling of pine. She loved the forest, he thought.

He needed to keep her close.

1921

4.

In late autumn of her nineteenth year, Evelynne went with her father and her brother Tomás by train to Washington, D.C., for business. The country, free now from the shadow of the Great War, was glazed with the promise of opportunity. Still somewhat quiet, Tomás had survived the trenches. This would be their first journey east since his return. Josef hoped the trip would be a triumph, a deepening of his financial holdings and a return to public life for Tomás after his service in foreign lands.

They left for the nation's capital two weeks early because Josef had published and bound a chapbook of Evelynne's poems. He went about selling her chapbook to all who would give him audience. He took them by train, north to south along the coast. They arrived in the great cities of the east, Boston, New York, Philadelphia, D.C., where he sold more than one thousand copies to booksellers and men of influence and especially their wives. On the multitrack south of Boston, Evelynne beheld the aftermath of a train wreck. Mangled track and crumpled cars overturned like the playthings of giants. She saw broken glass with human forms strewn like dolls from the torn roof of a passenger car. Her father walked among the wreckage, pale bodies at his feet. The impression was ghastly and lasting.

In the capital city, among the politicians and leading industrialists of his day, her father went about his business. He bartered cash for more cash, setting his teeth in the side of those who opposed him. Alone, Tomás and Evelynne witnessed his gloating over the largest copper deal in modern times, and she became a young woman while he pursued his dream to dig holes in the ground big enough to bury a city.

Upon their return, the old order set in.

He stood at the upper window of the Victorian. "You must never marry," he told her. "I need you." He spread his hand toward the frontier town below, out over the wooden surface scaffolds spread like a linear forest among the hills where mines carved tunnels in the earth.

She said nothing then. But one night in winter she confronted him in the private dining room, a room walled with African ebony floor to ceiling, where servants placed hand-embroidered linens and silver settings beside white china etched with blue flowers and birds. As she and her father ate duck adorned by red potatoes wrapped in bacon, steamed broccoli on the stalk, and mounds of melting butter, she said, "I'll marry. I'll marry whomever I please." Tomás was out at work on the high hill, directing the quarry men. Still, she was confident, her father's voice often tender with her, not rageful as he was with Tomás, ten years her senior. When Tomás had come home from the war her father had held him in his arms on the stoop for a very long while, the stiff body of his son unmoving, the face grave and eyes remote.

The Baron had found it extremely difficult to contain himself when Tomás was away at the western front. In his grief at how the army took everything from Montana without reserve, from boys and young men to horses beyond number, he'd lessened his own mare herd from a gaudy seven thousand to not more than nine hundred, selling to ranches in Idaho so as not to feel so great a sting at things taken, loaded, and sent east by track and rail and off to war. Too much a reminder of his own son a weapon in the grip of government. He'd spoken profusely of his fear of his son's death. She'd detected below his fear a love for which he had no words. But with Tomás back now, Josef kept him with a jealousy beyond forbearance, for the business, and told Tomás he too would never be allowed to go away again. Father and son seemed bound to each other as if by rope or barbed wire.

She knew their enmity had much to do with Catherine, the woman from St. Louis to whom Tomás had pledged himself after the war.

Across a span of oak table stained dark she let the words rise. Her father had his head down as he chewed. Sweat on his face, a dark vein at his forehead. The vein appeared to bend as the muscles of his jaw bunched and released. He stood suddenly, lunging forward as he braced one hand on the table and slapped her face so hard she went headfirst to the floor. On her knees she paused for a moment, feeling her cheekbone, the skin inflamed as if hit with a hammer. The sting of it enraged her, and when she rose he was back at his food, seated with his head down again.

"Halt your mouth," he mumbled, not looking at her.

"I'll do no such thing," she said. He clenched knife and fork in his fists. The image set her head afire and she leapt to the table on her hands and knees, screaming as she raked his face with her nails. Crouching over him, she watched his skin bleed. He threw his implements down and stood gripping her shoulders as she glared into his eyes.

Her furious face. War in the bones of her body, he thought. So unlike her mother.

"Don't ever strike me again," she said through clenched teeth.

He smiled then and when he released her, they both returned to their seats. Finally he laughed. He had blood on his face. She was one even he would have to reckon with. This he had not accounted for.

She brushed her hands on her dress and sat up, prim, like a lady. What men perceive is altered by their self-perception, she thought. Her face held the bruise for weeks. Her cheekbone felt ill to the touch for months. His face never quite absorbed the wound she'd given. Upon close inspection the lines were still visible the day he died.

5.

SOME DISTANCE FROM Butte, Evelynne and her brother rode along a corridor of poplar and black spruce in the mountains above the ranch house. She noticed his posture was more subdued since the war but still stately in the saddle, graced by a broad shoulder as much as the kindness of one who'd seen death in great measure and viewed people humbly. He could be stone with their father, but he was water with her.

She couldn't help but wonder at the changes she saw in him. Leaning forward in the saddle, she patted Chloe's shoulder. Still so lovely to the eye, she thought, and she paused, hugging the horse's neck as she whispered in her ear and fed her a lump of sugar.

"Lovely to the eye," she said aloud. Chloe snorted.

"What now?" said Tomás, teasing her.

When they came to a stop, they looked out over the land. They

were on the first rise above the ranch house. She had always preferred the ranch house to the house in the city, favoring its open
interior over the close-walled construction of the Victorian.
Their horses pulled bunches of grass and chewed in tandem.
"Lovely in limbs and lovely in eyes," Evelynne said. She palmed
another lump of sugar into the horse's mouth. Chloe nickered
and tossed her head.

"See how she plays?" Evelynne said, and Tomás winked.

When they flicked the reins and chirped out of the corners of
their mouths, the horses climbed the slight incline to the upper
meadow, where they trotted through high blond grass. The wind
combed the meadow before them. They slowed the horses to a
walk.

"Who wouldn't love sugar?" Tomás said. "But your horse
might not have any teeth when she's old."

"Who will?" Evelynne laughed. "Yours will be wooden."

Tomás jabbed her shoulder with his index finger. She smiled.
But his voice had a dull tone, where before the war and before he'd
lost Catherine his tone had contained a vibrant music. Catherine
had fulfilled a certain hope, Evelynne thought. With her loss, of
which Evelynne herself knew little, her brother had become mo-
rose, and something in his eye made her desire to shake the dark
coins from his body and see him breathe freely again.

They slacked the reins together. The horses put their heads to
the earth and ate. To the west the sun's track lay heavy in the sky
while the eastern line began to darken. He touched her forearm,
pointing his face down the draw behind them to where the ranch
house was bathed in light, a soft line of smoke on an eastward
slant from the chimney. They turned west again, the sun awash

on their faces, a cold sun bronzed behind a wing of cloud above the mountains.

He remembered when she had come into the world. He had sobbed and sobbed over his mother's death. At ten, the sphere of his mortal being had narrowed to a steel point, then his father had placed his sister in his arms. The miracle of her existence took his breath away.

"I'd give my life for you, Evelynne, if it was asked of me."

"I believe that," she said.

"I want you to live, to be free of this place," he said.

"I have no need to be away from you or Father."

He looked at her. "He'll never let you go."

Evelynne put her hand over Tomás's hand.

"He will, Tomás, when the time comes," she said. "He must."

"He won't," Tomás said, taking his hand from hers. His chest was turned inward, the shoulders forward, shoulder bones prominent. She thought his breath constrained, his face weary as he peered over the valley to the layered mountains. His hands, she noticed, gripped the horn of his saddle and went white.

"Catherine?" she said. She reached for his arm, but turning his head, he pulled away.

She wondered at the line of his face, aloof and gentle at once. "You don't know, do you, Evelynne?"

"Tell me," she said.

"Catherine left me."

"In St. Louis," Evelynne said. "She said good-bye."

"Do you know why?"

"Father said she took another suitor," she answered. "Even

with you back home, he brooded for months. I didn't know if either of you would heal."

In the distance a ridgeline creased the deep dark. A congress of stars appeared in the sky. "There is nothing left for me here," he said. "No fault of yours. Only Father's. Our failure, his and mine."

"Father's?" she questioned.

"His greed," he said. "Greed as far back as the blood runs. That and my fear of facing him and making him change."

"You're too hard on yourself, and him," Evelynne said.

He exhaled then, as if a weight was placed on him.

"He found out I loved her, then went to St. Louis, where her father was a butcher. Our father purchased the building across the street and put a butcher's shop on the ground floor. He ran prices down until her father went out of business. It didn't take six months. In the end our father met her father, telling him what he'd done before he ordered the man to leave St. Louis. 'Never let your daughter see my son again,' Father said. 'Gladly,' her father responded, and spat on Father's shoes. They might have fought to the death, but Father had men with him. He had the gall to tell me there was no need for him to kill the man. Catherine's family went to Texas. Father hoped we'd be unable to make contact, but she found me in the night and spoke to me."

"What did she say?"

"She said, 'I can never be with you.'

"In that final meeting she did not touch me. She shed no tears. She delivered her message and left. I never saw her again."

Evelynne clutched his arm.

"I want to kill him, Eve. I want to find him in his sleep and choke the breath from him." Tomás's face shook.

Tomás thought she shouldn't fully know the blackheartedness of men. For his part, he wouldn't let her. A hidden hatred in him begged for the light of day. This much she knew. Hatred for his father and himself. But what more? he thought. He pictured himself in the brothels of Europe and St. Louis and, worse still, the passages hidden from view in the very city of his birth, Butte. It wouldn't do for her to see men for what they were, animals who pass between light and dark with the ease of wind or weather. In Evelynne's face he saw pain, concern. He wished he could keep her from whatever lay ahead.

They kept silent for a while before the horses carried them back down the draw into the dark that led to the ranch house. They rode quietly. When the horses were put up for the night, he walked with her to the house, where at the door he released her. "Does a man good to think," he said.

As he walked back up into the trees, she touched a strand of her hair to her lips before she looked away. She mounted the stairs to her room, put on her nightclothes and stood at the window.

He had fought in the trenches of France. He'd returned with invisible wounds. We are disparate shards, she thought. Fragmented, violent. Alone. She worried that her brother might not come back to himself.

The great poets entered an abyss of disregard, she reasoned, and were lost to the world. And yet they rose. Her brother needed her now.

When she thought this way she sensed the presence of the

Almighty, intimate and formidable. Her task was to consume the dark and give light. Through the broad windowpane she beheld a brilliant black sky. The stars and their seasons. Scorpio, the Great Bear, Taurus, Orion. The Triangle and Cygnus. They burned, hardy, dauntless in the night.

6.

HER BROTHER WOULD not be comforted, and how could he? Evelynne thought. The events in St. Louis could not be made right. Evelynne's heart seemed to smoke in her chest. But he, her own brother, he needed to be made right. Her father was not as entrenched as Tomás might portray. He could be changed. He'd shown them the great cities of America. He'd supported her like a beloved benefactor. In fact, she saw him as such. Her recitations gave him gravity in every circle, from the bastions of financial providence to the women of high society here and in the east, even to the centers of government.

She had currency with him, she told herself. She thought of the life he'd made for her. By the age of twelve she had read much of his extensive library and by fourteen crafted an epic poem of heroic couplets that detailed a history of the modern French and American revolutions. By eighteen she'd become so enamored with Dickinson and Whitman that he'd openly wondered if she might not have the whole body of their work committed to memory. She knew Hopkins too, the poet priest long dead whose poems were fresh to Europe and America. She had asked her father on his travels to find and purchase through his array of connections signed originals of these poets whenever possible. In her bedroom he'd built a bookcase specifically for these. Her own chapbook had made a small sensation in New York City as well as abroad in Paris.

But it was not just her poetry, she thought. He loved her as well as he could. She was all that remained of her mother, and he had certainly loved her mother.

Evelynne knew him to be lonely. Like a body made of vapor, she thought.

She also knew he loved Tomás, though he treated Tomás harder. He'd made him a man, bold with other men and unafraid of power. If Tomás could forgive his father, then he'd carry the whole operation when their father was gone.

She knew it wasn't really that her father never wanted them to marry. It was just that he needed them. He was frail in his greed and not a little intemperate. She and Tomás could make their own way when the time was right, but the wait would not suffice for Tomás, she thought.

Her brother knew the lay of the land now, their father had shown them as much to make them understand the scale and scope of his business, which reached even to the splinter tracks on the northern Montana border near the Marias River, tracks that brought stores of copper north to the Empire Builder, then

all the way east and west. An idea bloomed in her mind. The
Marias country was home to wilderness, home to majesty and
awe. That land could set Tomás's mind at ease again. She'd take
Tomás there, she thought. Get him far away from their father
for a time.

In the dark of morning she rode from the ranch house back to
Butte, arrived at first light, and let the horse be stabled. She went
to her father at his desk, where he poured over figures and plans,
drawings of machinery and men, the movement of dirt, rock,
and mountains.

He looked up when she entered.

She went to him directly and put her head on his shoulder.

"Good morning, Father."

Outside the house a meadowlark sounded. Josef kept his eyes
on the pages before him. She left him to sit across from him in a
swivel chair made of walnut. Raising his eyes, he said, "I trust the
ranch is in order." He owned not only the ranch but the mountains that encircled the ranch.

"Yes," she said. "All is in order."

She sat still, her legs crossed in brown riding breeches with
leather inseams, a blouse of frilled silk, cream-colored, beneath
her riding jacket. She rested her hands on her lap. He saw her
hair, dark red with morning light, and her fine-boned face, and
he was reminded again of her mother. She cocked her head to
the side. She wanted something of him. Something of import.
Likely something he could not give, he thought.

"Speak," he said.

His anger, unwanted, rose like gorge in his throat.

"Thank you, Father," she said. Leaning forward, she placed her hands on his desk. Sculpted hands, he thought, like the Rodins of the Mastbaum collection in Philadelphia but more tapered, more refined. Her mother's hands. Efficacious and assured. Graceful.

"You've had a difficult night," she began.

"So I have," he said, staring at the table, her hands, the papers below her hands. She read him well. Always had. She wasn't pretentious. *Money is dirt*, she had told him recently. The gall of it. *Money is money*, he'd responded and she'd looked at him with pity. *Money is what keeps us alive.*

"I'm sorry," she said now, and he answered, "It's nothing," almost before she finished. She was devout like her mother. Often he didn't know what to do with her. His own upbringing had been fiercely biblical. He didn't chide her for her innocence.

"Do you value me?" she said.

Lifting his face to her, he said, "More than anything. You, your brother. All this." He waved his hand over the desk.

"Then why not let Tomás go?" Her eyes implored him.

"He's free to go. But here he has all he needs."

"You broke him in St. Louis."

He made a few stray marks on the paper with his drafting pencil. "He needed to be broken," he said.

"You don't believe that."

"I do," he said.

She put her hand on his forearm. "You'll lose him, then."

He set his face into her. "He'll remain here. He'll inherit it all. Everything here is his and yours."

"Surely you'll lose him, Father. Let him go so you don't have to."

Scowling at her, he removed her hand from his forearm.

"I will not," he said. His left hand was a fist. His right wrote jagged marks in his ledger, dark lines that looked like crows and meant nothing.

She rose to her feet, placed her hands on the desk again, leaning directly over him. Her mouth was not far from the line of his jaw. "He's gone from you already," she said.

"Enough," he said, placing his hands flat. He didn't let his voice rise. "He'll stay, as will you. Neither of you will go."

"Hear me," she said.

He felt her breath at the bone behind his ear. "He hates you," she said.

He turned to her then, hands gripping the edge of the desk. "His affection will return." He spoke with haste. His voice trembled. "Hate is love's underbelly. He'll return to me, as will you." His face seemed to say he had overcome her, but she redoubled her effort, setting her words into him like hooks.

"Did you hate Mother, then?"

He shook his head as if to ward her off. His mouth felt heavy.

"Why do you vex me, child?"

"You beg vexing," she replied. "You mix hate with love, but they separate like oil and water. With relish, you place kindling at your own son's feet. You set a match to him, and it rips your insides from you, yet you say nothing." Her voice notched upward. "All is not well! Day by day your soul is taken."

For a moment he seemed to deflate.

"My soul left me when your mother died," he said.

Evelynne touched his face. Water came to her eyes.

"If you don't change," she said, "you'll lose all you've ever loved."

His lips were tight. "I will lose nothing," he countered. "If he leaves, I can reach him anywhere."

His face was red now, the hair at his temples silver.

"Don't you see?" she said. "He doesn't want to leave. He just wants your decency. He wants to have a family of his own. He wants Catherine. Let him go to her. Make things right. You can return what was taken."

"Never," he said.

His words smote her. She receded.

"Others. Outsiders," he said as she moved away from him. "They want to steal what we have! I won't let them. I will never give back what was mine to take."

At the rail to the stairs she paused. "Tomás needs to be away from you, at least for a while. Let me bring him north to the operation there. I'll reason with him. See if he might be won again. I fear he will not. But let me help him."

He looked at her, the tilt of her head, her listening ear. "He must do his work like he did at Harvard. In St. Louis he wanted to escape until I brought him home. He's here now. Back from war. He knows the business. He must do his work."

"He will," she said, turning to him again. "I'll take him north for one year. You need to be away from each other. I assure you, he'll come back stronger."

When he saw that her eyes were very sad, he walked to her at the stair. "Who will watch over you?" he implored.

"Tomás," she answered. "I can write my poems there. The river and the terrain will be good for me."

He touched her shoulder but she stood back from him.

"Yes," he said. "Perhaps you're right. Perhaps a year will do us some good."

A year is all we need, she thought. We'll go to the operation on the Highline near the Marias River. Time will cleanse us.

That night she spoke with Tomás. Father and son did not speak.

Within the week she took Tomás north.

7.

EVELYNNE HELD TOMÁS'S hand and squeezed before she let it go. They sat across from each other, their heads angled some, their shoulders tilting forward or hitching back with the lifts and turns of the track. A gray tone to his eyes. There were shadows in the car before the sun appeared, fulminant over a broad draw flanked by mountains. The valley sat in a bowl atop the Great Divide. A high, wide land more handsome even than the Silver Bow from which they'd come. Butte they called home, but here they found a more rugged invention, the sheer mass and rock of a starker blend, thick forests with rivers like silver ore among them.

"We're away," she said, unfolding her white kerchief to give him a biscuit coated in butter.

"Thank you, Eve." Tomás met her gaze.

"My pleasure," she said.

He nodded, but she recognized the strain in him. They both

ate. There was more than loss in his face. He scared her with his surrender. A sense of submission. Nearly all her life she'd known only his poise and radiance.

He looked out the window. Shook his head. Drew his eyes to her again. "Eve, you're a godsend."

Unbeknownst to Tomás, against their father's will, she had tried to make contact with Catherine in Texas, seeking reparation through Chan. Return word had not yet come. She could not be certain, but intuitively she sensed that Chan kept their alliance in such things from her father. She wondered sometimes if Chan might not be an agent of heaven.

Tomás removed his own kerchief from his chest pocket. He gave it to her, and she wiped her fingers. They rode in silence for a time. Except for her, the compartment was populated solely by men. Her brother as well as four strangers. The other men surveyed her. She stared at Tomás as he faced the windows, watching the land. The buttered bread made her mouth water. She had not thought of her own shapeliness for some time. Mostly she thought little of herself, but she felt with near certainty that the other men looked on her here as if she were beautiful, and she blushed. Tomás seemed to sense what was at work in her. "Sister?" he said in a kind voice. "Do you feel alright?"

"Yes," she answered. "The air is heavy. Will you take me to the landing?"

"Certainly." He took her arm, and they walked the aisle to the back of the compartment, where he opened a wooden door. They stepped onto a metal surface encompassed by waist-high wrought-iron railings. Through the space between the cars the land rose and fell as the train pushed north. He didn't know how to be the brother he should be. My life is harmed rather than free, he thought, while she stands next to me bright-minded, pure of heart. She despises her own faults as much as she loathes wickedness. But men intrigue her. He admitted she desired their adoration, and in fact nearly beckoned them outright. Time in wilderness and on horseback had made her a woman. Love for her father and brother had made her divine. He placed his hand over hers.

When they returned to their seats, she hated to see her brother so silent. She knew he was a good man, but men as a whole were a mystery, and when their eye turned her way, here or in the city, she witnessed in them even more than she bargained for. Quiet, covetous looks from some, from others a kind of hardening of the eyes and uplift of the posture, something like ownership or payment on what they thought one day to own. She would not be owned by any man. Scolding herself for her vanity, she told herself to stop thinking of men.

"We did it," she said to Tomás.

"Did what?"

"Gave you space, Tomás. Room to breathe."

"Who did it?" he said. "Him?" Anger in his voice.

"You and I," she said, and Chan too, she thought. She believed Chan had helped her father open himself toward Tomás.

He let his shoulders down. "It was you, Eve, I know," he said. "I'm grateful."

They took the train on the branch line to their holdings in the north. In the early-morning darkness, he had commandeered the animals, walking them aboard on a ramp.

At the final stop she and Tomás disembarked on a high mountain plain. They followed the short line of the train back to the horse car. There he walked them down the loading ramp out on open ground. The horses shook their manes and ate for a good long while. Evelynne put her face to Chloe's shoulder. Breathing in, she placed her arm around the horse's neck. The sweetgrass smell of the coat was an inebriation she never tired of. She moved from Chloe to Tomás's horse, brushing her hand on the horse's rump as she said sweet things. Tomás looked off into the distance. She noticed the downward lean of his left shoulder, the slant of his body slightly out of kilter from how her father had run him over with the oxcart.

The workmen began to saddle the horses. She approached Tomás and slipped her arm into his. "We're here now, Tomás," she said. "All will be well."

"Yes, Evelynne," he said, the sonority of his voice distinctly like his father's.

She mounted, placed her hands on the pommel, and watched the ridgeline. Behind it the ramparts of the mountains were like citadels. The eye was led down through quaking aspen and cottonwood to the banks of the Marias, where water brimmed at the roots of trees before flowing on a wide berth west below Wolf's Pass.

THEY HAD COME to a place lush and elemental, where granite rose to crown the continent and sun flared over swaths of snow in the heights of the mountains. Windblown. Isolate. Their father's empire would lay track here and finally on the ascent through the most useful pass northward toward the Highline. This would connect them to the railway called the Empire Builder. In its entirety the new line would run from the Empire Builder south along the Continental Divide to Butte, where one of the northern hemisphere's greatest storehouses of copper could be unearthed and sent to market. The track they'd ridden would meet the northern offshoot within the month. The middle of the state would then be connected, a grid of infrastructure west to Seattle, Portland, San Francisco, and Los Angeles and east to St. Paul, Chicago, and New York. A line north in Montana to match the line south. The copper output would double overnight.

The world pulsed with insight and industry, the nations of the world hungry like animals. Their father, the Baron Josef Lowry, vowed to keep the nations fed. She had seen his face enraged over those in his command, his forehead a net of veins. All increased in drive and design under his ambition. Nothing decreased or stagnated. If it threatened delay, he cut it off like a gangrenous limb. He would earn his millions. But he had a premonition, in the end those who followed him would make him minuscule. More fully than he ever imagined, in the seventy years after the Baron Josef Lowry's passing, others would capitalize on a hole in the earth that yielded seven million tons of copper worth three hundred billion dollars. Their names would be Rockefeller and Rogers. Amalgamated Copper would give birth to the behemoth Anaconda Copper Mining Company. Lowry's name would be forgotten. The men who followed him would be conquerors.

Josef a mere blazer of trails.

8.

THEY RODE THE horses north, the truncated track behind them
a memory of their father's appetite and impatience. Tomás
wore a red neckerchief and his bone-colored Stetson with the
rolled rim. For Eve, a small black derby with a white silk scarf.
Her long coat and riding breeches. Her braid down her back.
At dusk they entered base camp on the rise that overlooked the
blend of two waters where Ten Mountain River gleamed in sun
as it emptied into the Marias like a shaft of light into the darker
flow. The operation went on above the confluence eastward
into a cleft in the mountains where the men returning to camp
spilled from the gap, walking toward Evelynne and Tomás.
Their large hands hung like mallets at their sides. Their heads
on the approach blocked the light. The faces of the workers
were narrow or round, hard boned or deep set, with white eyes
that peered out from visages blackened by dirt, a small army
of European immigrants, Irish, German, Czech, Norwegian,

some French. Those from China in wide circular hats and thin braids walked with a sturdy gait like strange two-legged pack animals. Tomás tipped his hat while he and Evelynne rode forward quietly. The immigrant men put a hand to their broken work caps, nodding as they passed.

She pondered over what she felt to be the virtue of men who spent labor for a wage, their strength in leg and shoulder, their wide chests and broad backs. Some were big, very big. Other men were small. Still others wiry. There were fighters here, she thought, and men of some gentility, in with those who lived below other men. She slowed her horse, asking Tomás to slow with her. The horses came to a halt as the last of the men passed through the darkness beside them, on toward shelters made of wood and canvas, large old military tents stocked with cots and a woodstove.

As they gave heel, the horses moved up the embankment. She was invigorated, happy to be with Tomás here in this land where men sought to tame the untamable. When Tomás glanced at her, she thought she saw peace in him. She clicked her tongue in the dim light, leading the horses on to the overseer's tent.

The two dismounted, then walked to the triangle opening. Under the brim of his hat, the overseer's face was illumined by the stove fire. The man rose, his face passing again to shadow as he went with them across a spate of rocky ground toward the platform structure kept for her father on his visits. They mounted three stairs and entered the dwelling that was her father's base of operation, a framed rectangle with a wood floor. The rafters angled in pairs from the apex to the wall vertices. Canvas roof with canvas walls. The overseer had set a blaze in the stove. The smell of tamarack and lodgepole came from the fire along with the high scent of sap, pungent as it released from the wood.

"Fired the stove for you, sir," he said to Tomás while he tipped the brim of his hat to Evelynne. "Ma'am."

"Thank you," Tomás said as Evelynne nodded. The overseer closed the door behind him with a softness befitting her presence. She felt a kinship for him and for all her father's men here in this bed of wilderness.

9.

AFTER DARK THE sound of coyotes like wailing women carried the night. When they quieted, she fell asleep but later a wolf on the mountain issued a lone note, bent and haunting, that startled her awake. She crept from her cot near the stove, approaching her brother's form where he lay on his bedroll on the other side of the room. He slept with his back turned to her. Leaning forward, she went to one knee and saw hardness in his face and crease lines on his forehead. His eyes were pinched shut. She placed her hand on his shoulder. When he didn't wake she whispered over him. "Who has believed our message, and to whom has the arm of the Lord been revealed?" He breathed once, sharply, before exhaling. She kept her hand on his shoulder as she finished her prayer.

His face did not change, but his body calmed, the rise and fall of his chest, the ease of his frame in sleep. She made the sign of the cross over him and rose, listening. The night had gone still.

She stood in the center of the room. No sound of insect or animal, nor even the wind. She walked back to the cot and tucked herself in. The stove still harbored a slow burn. She pictured the embers hollowed, blue bleak fire brought to life by a breath.

She slept, and she dreamed.

She dreamed of a river, a muscled arm roiling from the mountains to the plains, where it smoothed itself and went serene, meeting the sun at the far curve of the earth. She was a bird alive, mighty of wind and wing, and as she flew over the land she saw the water, a glimmering line beneath her. She gave a cry that pierced the sky while she turned her wings, sweeping upward over the heights of the mountains and back again on a long curve to the source, to the headwaters. Far below her a large lake lay like a blue eye in the bowl of the mountains. Earth, cloud, and rock, the white of atmosphere, the ache of torque upon weft of wing, flight, darkness, descent. When she entered the water, she sped deep down. The dream dispersed. She slept until dawn.

On this day Tomás would begin work on the tracks her father's men had commenced through the pass. She lay still, thinking of Chan's knowledge, a fount of discernment regarding trains and men. He was her father's clerk, and though other men thought it folly, and though Chan was paid no more than a pittance, he was her father's most trusted business ally. Chan spoke of Asa Whitney, the American businessman who had gone to China and been taken by the vision of a railroad across the United States in order to secure the trade of the Orient. Whitney imagined railroads. Now the whole country was rife with them. The Golden Spike of 1869 brought engine Jupiter of the Central

Pacific Railroad together with Number 119 of the Union Pacific Railroad. When they kissed, the first transcontinental railway was born. "Once the threshold was transcended," Chan had told her, "four more transcontinentals followed by 1885."

Before Whitney, stagecoaches and pony express riders, wagons over the west. Now the iron horse. Chan knew the world, Josef credited him with that and therefore sought his counsel on affairs, but for Evelynne, Chan's true gift was in helping her understand the wiles of people, the dangers with the ingenuities. He imparted wisdom no one else knew, from various sources: her father's circles of influence, letters from Chinatown, newspapers Chan ordered monthly from New York City and San Francisco, Singapore and Hong Kong. She thought him strong-hearted, with the mind of a genius. *Your spirit is for him*, he had said. Her spirit. To console her brother's spirit and draw him up from darkness.

Today her brother would direct men and engines. Evelynne would accompany him. Tomás needed her. She'd stay with him until the work was done.

10.

IN THE MORNING they entered the mountains, the horses driving upward through the pass. A Monarch butterfly tilted among the trees where they rode, Evelynne marveling over the black-and-umber inlay of its wings. Not far on she heard the boom of rail work, a blasting that commenced at sunrise on a daily turn until dark. The ground the workers gained was scant but steady.

The overseer walked the line and directed the positioning of iron spikes pounded into the rock in advance of the laid track. The spikes quilled outward at an angle into which sticks of dynamite were set. The men gained distance, fanning down the corridor before each blast. The efficiency impressed her, the workers' faces appearing bruised in the shadows of morning, the men from the evening before and others now, Swedes and Poles and some few Russians, their look more ruddy, thick-boned and square-jawed—the far-northern Europeans drawn to the upper tracts of a newly charted country. She hoped they'd find what they sought. A living, Tomás said, perhaps enough money to purchase a small piece of land.

The men of China were different, together and of their own pace, they worked with a movement precise and machine-like. Though she knew they were paid on paltry terms, they held their heads impassive. Their resolve and achievement she likened to the bear who moved light on padded paws alive to the wilderness. Long black braid down the midback to the waist, plain clothes, a flat circumference to their hats, their faces pallid, it appeared to her they worked without ceasing.

Tomás rode in front of her. When younger he had always gone before her into the fray with a light heart, shouting for her to come with him. Delighted, she followed, among the clay hills on horseback or down to the river where they tied a rope to the branch of a cottonwood and flew into the water.

Their father once had a wife to pull the light of day up through him, she thought. In like fashion she had done the same for her father as a child, just as Tomás had done for her, but now Josef had grown increasingly august, his manner eclipsed by the empire within his reach, though she didn't believe her father truly wanted what he claimed.

Beneath his ambition was self-hatred, she thought. Her brother rode ahead of her in the pass. She beheld the bud of a similar absence in him, in the lean of his body in the saddle and the turn of his head, yet without their father's callousness. He dismounted and walked forward, standing beside the overseer while the men removed a spike the length of a forearm and placed a bundle of dynamite in the hole. A hundred men worked in the distance north securing track to ground, and now a small grouping

of six just ahead of her approached in the dim light, removing
their crumpled felt hats as they passed her by, saying "Ma'am,"
and "Come back, Ma'am."

"Dynamite in the hole Ma'am," they said as the overseer
came on, leading her brother's horse, the animal supple and
black with some white in the foot. Her face questioned the
overseer. "He's with the dynamiter," he said as he passed by,
motioning her down and away. She backed her horse until she
came even with the overseer. She ran her hand along the neck
of Tomás's horse. In the distance she saw the candle flare of the
wick. Tomás and the lightman moved toward her, Tomás carrying the spike. The wick died then, causing the men to pause
and go back. They both looked in the hole again, but when the
lightman set the flame a second time the blast was immediate.

She recoiled, throwing her arm over her face.

Above the cloth of her sleeve she witnessed fire from the blast
hole as the bodies of Tomás and the lightman lifted to the sky.
The bodies tilted and in the end fell as if punched back to earth.
A storm of rubble followed. She screamed Tomás's name as
men ran from behind her into the gap. She quieted, then grew
completely still, grit on her face, a shawl of dust on her shoulders. The overseer first, then many more came on, moving rock
and soil as they sought to uncover the bodies. She brought her
horse up, the animal's eyes and forelegs furtive, picking her way
among scattered debris. Her face shook. She kept her fists firm.

In the acrid afterburn of the explosion her nose tingled. The
horse did not want to be here but she muscled the reins and
spoke in a hard tone. "Stay put! Steady." Her voice seemed dislodged from her mouth, as if the words were not connected to

her or were not hers at all but rather small black birds that darted into the sky. She drew the horse still. Her heart would break the bones in her chest, she thought. "Tomás," she said as she eyed the rock and the collapsed mountain wall. A sharp bend of fear started low, building to a howl inside her.

They discovered the lightman first, his head and hair encased in broken earth, the countenance a mask of dirt, his mouth and eyes closed. His face appeared powdered with brown chalk. Dead as if he'd never lived. When they lifted him from the trappings of the mountain, his body hung in their arms like cloth.

Her brother lay deeper. When the men removed the last level of rock, she stood beside the overseer. A dark bloom colored the ground behind her brother's head. His hat was nowhere to be found. The spike had taken part of his skull and was still embedded at an angle through his jaw out the top of his head. The overseer covered her face with his hat. As she fell on his shoulder darkness closed around her.

She didn't wake until she felt the bump and jolt of the train.

Night, she pressed her cheek to the glass, a wide valley among mountains out the window. The sky imprinted with stars. All was uncommonly vivid below, the open span of grasses unmoving as if cast in silver, the forest and the bulk of the mountain appearing sepia, metallic, and blue. Above, over the whole world, blackness. The stars are not our own, she thought. We are nothing.

The overseer sat across from her. She did not give him her eyes. When we leave this place, she thought, no one knows our name.

"My brother?" she said.

"Draped in the car behind us," he said.

II.

SHE MADE IT through the funeral, her father like a statue over the open grave, Chan's elderly frame in the distance beside the base of a giant oak. She found the coffin's satin finish with copper appointments hideous among the hard earth and granite that towered over them.

Weeping aloud, she gripped her father's waist.

In the end he nearly carried her in his arms to the carriage. They drove in silence to the ranch house.

The Baron steeled his mind against grief and never spoke of his son's death. Fortifying himself, he pointed his face ahead.

Evelynne's sorrow, though, could not be satiated. A hole had been carved in her that grew and would not be closed. There in the mountains she chose a solitary life, wholly dividing herself from the city and people. At the ranch, if she was not out riding or walking seemingly for days on end in the wilderness, she kept to her room. She put her own mount away, forbidding the horse to be ridden. She could not bear to gaze upon Chloe's face, the eyes so resolute and knowing. If she rode, she rode her father's horse, but most often she preferred walking.

Word from Catherine never came.

Evelynne was not seen in public for years.

BLACK KETTLE, 1864

12.

A YEAR IN the cauldron of civil war. In a time of severity and struggle, Black Kettle, chief of six hundred Cheyenne, led his people following buffalo along the Arkansas River of Kansas and Colorado. They passed through the scablands of the north, rock outcroppings with veins of sage, swells of sparse grass that led finally to a land broken by coulees where a few thin cottonwoods remained even in the dry dirt. The trees looked barely alive, waiting on storms or flash floods. When Black Kettle saw their withered form, he continued on, bringing the Cheyenne to Big Sandy Creek in the Colorado territory. Though they had no signed treaty, he and his people relied on goodwill. They camped near the white man's outpost called Fort Lyon, where he meant to make peace and accept sanctuary.

JOHN CHIVINGTON, HIS family having immigrated to America some generations before, raised the Third Colorado Cavalry, a hodgepodge militia mixed equally of drunkenness and the wish to kill. Chivington led a force of seven hundred men into Fort Lyon, giving notice of his battle plan against the nearby Cheyenne encampment. Although informed that the Cheyenne under Black Kettle had already surrendered, Chivington left the garrison in order to direct his men to pursue Cheyenne extinction.

BLACK KETTLE LAY in the lodge on a bed of sagebrush covered with robes, the warmth of his wife like a bird in the palm. He remembered in former days how the band had asked to be brought as blood into the white man's family. He had been a young soldier chief then. As he'd listened to the head chief he'd thought the request very wise: the chief had asked the white leaders for one thousand white women to be given as brides to the Cheyenne, to unite the Cheyenne with the white man. The white man, haughty, had refused.

Black Kettle's camp meandered along the Big Sandy, one hundred twenty lodges, people of skeletal hunger, sunken eyes, and burnished skin, near dead, he thought. For them, he held both hope and great despair. He remembered a time when dogs licked antelope grease from the tips of his fingers and he rubbed his hands in the scruff of their fur. There were no dogs now. Everything seemed to be made of starvation or war.

Not two winters before, at dusk on a plateau over the big river, he saw a buck on the edge of the forest, head high, wearing a circular crown of ten tines. The buck stood, ears alert, harem of seven does flowing like water around him. Black Kettle smelled the rut of them from across the river. *"Ha Ho!"* Black Kettle shouted so the buck perked to him before leaping away, bounding along the tree line as the does followed. Black Kettle smiled, their tails like white flags, flying as they ran.

In the darkness now, Black Kettle rose and walked among the sleeping lodges. A strong village once, but now with so much hunger Black Kettle's sorrow was heavy. He had fought wars with the white man at Fremont's Orchard, Cedar Canyon, and Buffalo Springs, where the soldiers had killed Chief Starving Bear. Black Kettle had made raids along the overland routes and killed the Hungates at Box Elder Creek. He had killed Marshall Kelly, capturing his white woman, Laura, near Little Blue River. But the white man only increased in number and took more Cheyenne lives. He walked the full length of the village along the north side of Sand Creek. He heard the sound of the river. He was glad no one rose to greet him. The night revealed the shadow figure of a black bear on the far hill, walking. Black Kettle sang his chief's song, for he would do a good thing tomorrow; he'd take the people all the way into the white fort to make peace so they might not starve.

The time was not the same as former times, like when Wolf Tooth and the Cheyenne made peace with the Utes. Then they just came together, each man choosing a friend on the other side to give gifts. Clothing and moccasins, a horse or two. In this way Wolf Tooth had gained a Kiowa friend who had given him a strong horse and some beautiful clothes along with those good moccasins the Kiowas wore with leather soles all in one piece and fringes on the heel and on top. Wolf Tooth had given the Kiowa man all his best clothes in return, with an excellent war horse he hated to give up, but he was happy to have a friend in the tribe they used to fight.

The whites were different. They gave as a group, clothing, calico, flour, sugar. Coffee. One time they butchered a hundred head of cattle by a river, but the white men let the meat sit too long. The Cheyenne never touched those carcasses but just let them rot because the meat tasted funny. It was too sweet, so they wouldn't eat it.

At the end of camp Black Kettle stood, watching the river. In a meadow across the water One Eye's brown-and-white paint, a fast, fearless horse, stared back at him. Black Kettle returned to his lodge and lay down. Drawing his wife near again, he held her as she slept and he waited for sleep. The white men troubled him. They do not love the sound of their own mothers' names, he thought.

Deep and dark the dream. Darker the waiting day.

13.

BLACK KETTLE RAISED an American flag and a white flag of peace over his tipi.

Chivington quieted his men.

He sat astride a big-haunched pale horse on hardscrabble dirt under the gray predawn sky. He was thick in the face with beady deep-set eyes, a small ingrown beard, and a wide nose. Chivington positioned his men, along with their four howitzers, around the Cheyenne village of Black Kettle. "I've come to kill Indians," he said. "I believe it's right and honorable to use any means under God's heaven to kill Indians." Chivington, nicknamed the Fighting Parson, was presiding elder of Denver's First Methodist Episcopal Church.

"Remember boys, big and little. Nits grow up to make lice. Kill them all."

Scream of gunfire in the waking hour. The shouts of warriors.

The wails of women and children running in the half dark over the surface of the water. They went to the far side of the river to make of it a small barrier between the charge of the white man on foot and horseback, the soldiers filled with bloodlust for the ill-prepared. A small band of warriors put up return fire with bow and arrow and some few guns, making time for Black Kettle to move with those he could, following the children through the water.

Behind Black Kettle white men walked like darkness painted pale. Their weapons were rifles and bayonets, knives and hatchet blades and axes. They used big guns in smoking towers rolled on wheels, spitting fire on the body of the Cheyenne.

Below him in the riverbed, Black Kettle's wife fell, shot multiple times in the back. Beyond her the white interpreter William Bonner and his wife, Magpie, Black Kettle's own niece, emerged from their lodge near the southern point of camp. A big man with red hair, hands raised, he waived his arms. "Stop!" he shouted. "Halt!" But the white men pushed him aside, and Chivington rode over him where he stood. Black Kettle thought how like a windblown tree the man looked, angled toward the ground, arms askew as the horse bowled him over. The sharp scent of cannon powder on the wind, the hands of the attackers made hard circles in the air as they struck children, shot old men, and kneeled in fierce strokes over women, the white men with vigorous knife work who sawed roughly and desecrated the dead.

Black Kettle faced uphill, shouting, "Fly! Keep alive! We gather after nightfall!"

AS THE CANONS and rifles pounded the Cheyenne, Chivington rode engulfed by men drunk on liquor and blood, rushing down on those who asked for restraint. But he wanted no prisoners. The group of warriors holding the river ran through the water, then up the hillside. They followed the few who escaped. Near the far bank a single dead tree, white as bone and nearly limbless, stood in stark contrast to the black water. A lantern moon hung low in the early morning dark, touching the land with opaque light. Over the battlefield winds sent a flock of black swifts swerving. They banked upward along the river before they fell away, reckless with speed.

CHIVINGTON PRESSED FORWARD and blew the people from their moorings. When he stopped he held up his arm for his men to halt, then dismounted and took them on a tour of the dead. He jerked each head taut, carving away their hair before he opened their deerskin clothes. He set his hand on their genitals and scalped women's pubic hair. He cut off their breasts. He took the genital skin of boy and man to use and sell, coin pouches for the privileged. Fine place, he thought, to carry what economy a man might have. The men followed him, spitting epithets, gathering what they could. They pocketed grotesque treasures. They choked on laughter, busy building frenzy to nightfall, when they grouped to build their fires, conflagrations that licked like tongues, phosphorescent orange and red in the hovering dark.

OUTSIDE DURING THE long night, the remnant of the Cheyenne smoldered on the plain. Finally they rose, moving like smoke, children of the day who bore silently the massacre that turned women to warriors and made every Cheyenne man pledge his life to kill the white man.

BLACK KETTLE'S WIFE was shot nine times and left for dead. Black Kettle took her up and carried her to where he found refuge in the camp of the Cheyenne Dog Soldiers at Smoky Hill River. From that day forward she was called Woman Hereafter. Black Kettle lay down with his wife again in the healing lodge. In her face he found a depth of darkness he had never before seen. Try as he might, he could not awaken her voice. He lay next to her, pressing his cheek to hers. He heard her breath, shallow and ragged in the hollow of her body. She gripped his hand. He held her.

INTO THE DARK Chief Leg-in-the-Water said, "What do we want to live for? The white man has taken our country and killed all of our game. He was not satisfied with that but killed our wives and children.

"Now no peace.

"We want to go and meet our families in the spirit land. We loved the whites until we found out they lied to us and robbed us of what we had.

"We have raised the battle ax until death."

14.

IN AN AVENGING wildfire the warriors gathered and healed their wounds. They rose with vindicated eyes to find and kill white people, so that on a day not long after Sand Creek they entered the battle of the Little Bighorn in southeast Montana territory, where they took the gold-headed leader of the white men, called Custer, and kissed the earth with his blood.

This they did in the traditional way; the lowest and weakest among them gave their lives.

FROM THE CHEYENNE, four men. The poorest ones with no guns, only bow and arrow, club and hatchet. Owning little, having won little honor, the four made a vow to the people: "In our next engagement with the white man, we fight until we die."

Whirlwind, son of Black Crane. Noisy Walking, son of White

Bull or Ice. Cut Belly. Closed Hand. The suicide boys of the Cheyenne.

The dying dance was prepared. When the men entered the circle, the people cheered, celebrating their courage. The men danced all night, the reckless way, hued with paint both white and dark as blood, dancing until morning, when they emerged and went out through a camp of eight thousand Cheyenne, Sioux, and Arapaho, spread four miles along the river.

When they walked, the old men walked on either side of them. The criers called out in a loud voice. "Look at these men for the last time. Today they are alive. Today they throw their lives away."

THE CHEYENNE FOUR joined suicide warriors from the Sioux, and together they went with the war party to the field of war, diving on horseback into the enemy's final position. They flew as the spear point, piercing the enemy. They fought hand to hand until they died at gunpoint as the larger mass of warriors flowed in behind, killing Custer, routing his white soldiers, killing them all.

Sitting Bull and Crazy Horse with the combined forces of the Cheyenne, the Lakota Sioux, and the Arapaho orchestrated an advance that left Custer and his two hundred men dead in less than an hour. A battle of two fronts, one on either side of a winding ridge, the warriors ran the distance between, decimating their enemies.

Over two valleys of dead men, blue sky.

15.

LONG DAYS PASSED before Chivington was brought to justice. William Bonner, the white interpreter who had lived with the Cheyenne the day of the massacre, was actually a half-breed. Half Welsh, half Cheyenne, a redheaded giant of a man. His father had been named William too. Bonner was married to the Cheyenne woman called Magpie, Black Kettle's cousin. At Sand Creek Bonner lost consciousness, and when he woke with broken ribs, his innards punctured, he found his wife dead beside him, her body mutilated. This man reported Chivington's deeds and brought Chivington to trial.

Chivington's command was removed, his run for office derailed.

But Chivington lived a long life.

The interpreter William Bonner raised his children alone and died in sorrow, still mourning the death of Magpie.

ZION, 1907

16.

EIGHT YEARS OLD and big, bull child, his father called him, and bulls he rode, starting at five on the old gray bull his father owned, then at six years and seven in the open fields of neighboring ranches. His mother named him Zion. He entered his first real rodeo at thirteen in Glasgow. Afterward, too big already for bulls, he turned to steer wrestling in Glendive and Billings and on from there, three broken fingers, a broken ankle, broken clavicle and cracked wrist bone. Otherwise unharmed, he knew the taste of blood, fought men twice his age while going to bars with his father. When he lost, his father grew quiet, cussed him when they got home, beat him. When he won, his father praised him.

His solace in the outside world was his father's uncle, Bertrand, an old horseman gentle with animals who lived two miles off in a small log house. Though Bertrand talked little, he had kind eyes and taught the boy to handle horses. He was spry, barrel-chested with strong hands, but on a fall day when the boy brought firewood, he found his uncle dead in a draw a short distance from the cabin.

The boy retrieved his father. They spent the afternoon turning up earth for burial.

"Work," the boy's father said. "Because you ain't getting nothing. People are takers. As well shoot you as look at you."

At school the boy had high marks. He desired to please his mother.

Home, he smelled the gun-cleaning, the oil, the parts in neat rows on the kitchen table. The family inhabited a one-room ranch house: mother, father, son. There was a plank floor, an eating space, a bed space, cookstove. A small slant-roofed barn stood east of the house where the livestock gathered in the cold. Mother at the table, said, "Don't make a mess." Zion's father, meticulous, answered. "Quiet, woman." Outside, the flat of the high plains arced toward Canada. To the south the wild wind blew snow from here to a haze at the earth's end. A rim of sun, westerly, was red as blood.

The boy's mother read aloud by lamplight. Fire in a tube of glass. Looking up, into his eyes, "Mind your schooling," she said. She touched his face. The words she read went out far, they encompassed the world, and in the evening quiet Zion and his father curled at her feet on the bed, listening. "Before I formed you in the womb I knew you," she read to them, "and before you were born I set you apart."

His father never called him by name.

17.

Sixteen years old, Zion strode the fence line in a white-out. He was already six feet three inches tall. He weighed two hundred thirty pounds. Along a slight game trail he was north of the house in thirty below zero weather. He was searching for his father, gone three days. His father had come back from town with a flat look on his face. He'd sat on the bed and wouldn't eat. At dark he'd made a simple pronouncement, "Getting food," then gripped the rifle, opened the door and strode outside long-legged against the bolt of wind and snow. Gone.

Walking, Zion saw the black barrel of the rifle angled on the second line of barbed wire, snow a thin mantle on the barrel's eastward lie. He saw beneath it the body-shaped mound, brushed the snow away with a hand, found the frozen head of his father, the open eyes dull as gray stones. A small hole under the chin was burned around the edges. At the back of his father's head, fist-sized, the boy found the exit wound.

When he pulled the gun from his father's hand, two of the fingers snapped away and landed in the snow. Zion opened his father's coat, put the fingers in his father's front shirt pocket. He shouldered the body, carried the gun, took his father home. The boy's face was a tangle of deep-set lines. Where he walked, the land ran to the end of the eye until it met a sky pale as bone.

They put him on the floor under the kitchen table. At the gray opening of dawn Zion placed him in a bank of snow east of the barn, covering the snow with a blanket and a few branches.

At first thaw he spent morning to evening, using his father's pickax, then the shovel. Still they buried the body shallow. He pushed the earth in over his father, malformed rock fused with ice and soil, pounding the surface with the flat back of the shovel. The loud bangs sounded blunt and hard in the cold. A light snow still lingered, driven by wind on a slant from the north. His mother formed a crude cross of root wood from the cellar, which the boy took, manipulating the rock in order to position the cross at the head of the grave. Zion removed his broken felt cowboy hat, his gloves. His mother reached to hold his hand. Their faces turned raw in the cold. "Dead now," she said. "Your father saw the world darkly, and people darker still. Find the good, Zion." She squeezed his hand. "Dust to dust. May the Good Lord make the crooked paths straight. He makes the mountains to be laid low and the valleys to rise. May He do with the dead as He wills."

18.

INSIDE THE BOY a will was growing, abstruse, sullen, a chime-
ra of two persons, the man of violence at odds with the angel
of peace. Find the good, Zion thought, but then the sheriff and
banker came and said, "I'm sorry." The four rode in the cab of
the Studebaker back to town. Papers and words, the smell of wet
ink, the ranch was taken, some little money granted, and mother
and son moved thirty miles to Sage, farther yet toward the north-
east edge of Montana, the town joined to the straight rail track
that ran the Highline. Small town, Sage. Post office, two bars,
general store. They roomed with an old woman near dead in a
house with floors that shone of maple. Neat-lined hardwood in
every room.

At night a howling wind blended to the whistle of the long
train, the ground rumble of the tracks, the walls like a person
afraid, shaking, the bed moving. The bones in him jarred, but
as he listened he drifted, asleep, lost on a flatboard bunk near

the ceiling in a dark compartment, carried far into forested lands.

Within the year, the boy's mother died. In the morning under cover of cotton sheet and colored quilt he found her quiet and still. He laid himself down next to her. Holding her frail body in his arms, he shook silently. In the end he stood. Leaning over, he kissed her forehead. In her hair, the small ivory comb given by the boy's father nearly two decades before. Zion placed the comb in his breast pocket. In her hand he found a page torn from scripture, Isaiah, in her fingers of bone, the hollow of her hand, the place that was home to the shape of his face.

Zion waited, not knowing what to do. Behind the Bucking Horse Bar one night, he beat a man fresh from the rail line until the man barely breathed. It started when he cussed the boy, calling him outside. Zion followed, not caring. The man's face was clean, white as an eggshell, but Zion made it purple, a dark oblong bruise engorged above the neckline. There would be more fights, he knew, and when death came like the hand of an enemy, he'd give himself over, he thought, for it was death he desired and death he welcomed.

He lay on the hardwood floor at the house in Sage watching the elderly woman as she entered the front door. She was methodical as she turned the handle with tangled fingers. "Welcome, ma'am," he mouthed the words. "Same to you, boy," she answered. Same hour each day she returned from her small work at the general store.

It was dusk. He saw the woman's face, the boned-out look she wore. They had their greeting, she passed into the kitchen, he noticed the light, a white form reflected left-center in the front window. The old woman's house faced away from the town's main street. The reflection was a quirk, he thought, from the hollow globe-shaped lamp across the street beneath which the night people ebbed and flowed on the boardwalk. The light came through the aperture of a window at the top of the back stairs, hitting a narrow gold-framed mirror in the hallway, sending its thin icon into the wide living room. He heard the woman on the stairs, her languid gait, the creaking ascent to her room. She passed, the light disappeared, then returned.

19.

A MAN WILL be physical, he thought, forsake his kin, himself, the ground that gave him life. Death will be the arms to hold him. Zion curled inward, lay on the floor for days. Out on the flats, tumbleweeds rolled in the wind and stacked the fence lines. A dry openness led from town to the end of the earth. Small ears of cactus no bigger than his hand littered the expanse.

The greeting remained the same, the woman left him his space. In his brief life a single circus had passed through town. His father had taken him. Still on the floor, he pictured the electric bulb over the general store, pictured himself beneath it in the dirt street where he stood in the deep night looking up. Then he saw himself above it, behind it, clenching the roof between his knees as he would a circus horse, his chest upraised, his father's big sledgehammer lifted overhead. He pulled down sky with arms like wedges. He blasted the light to smithereens. He slept. Outside, he heard the loud confidence of the train engine, the steel wheels of the cars at high speed along the rails. In the early morning the old woman put a hand on his shoulder. The touch awakened him. He thought of his mother's hands, her nails thin and low in their beds, and he remembered how she worried them with her teeth. He'd tried not to look at them in her presence but rather to look at her whole hand, of a shape as dainty as a bird. He thought of gray-white birds. He thought of sparrows. Yes, he thought, I will leave this place.

The next day he rose, the old woman's horse beneath him, her gift to him. He moved south until he met the Missouri Breaks, where the land was bare on top but wrinkled like an old sheet in the fissures where pine and juniper grew. He passed through rugged undergrowth. He took a sharp slant south and west. Finally he came to Bozeman. No jobs. But, big, he got work in a feed store.

He wrestled steers in every rodeo he could find. Nearly every Saturday night he fought in bars. He didn't drink. He sought only the concave feel of facial structure, the line of a man's nose, the loose pendulum of the jawbone and the cool sockets of the eyes. He liked these things, the sound they made as they gave way, the sound of cartilage and how the skin slit open before the blood began. But he hated himself that he liked it.

Still, in the half dark of the bar in the basement of the Wellington Hotel outside White Sulphur Springs he opened the curve of a man's head on the corner of a table. A small mob gathered seeking revenge, the man's brothers, the man's friends. He threw them back and busted the teeth from the mouth of one. He broke the elbow of another. "You'll leave here dead," he said, and the group receded, the anger in him vital and full, and he walked from the open door alone into darkness until he sat off distant wrapping his knees in his arms, clenching his hands.

He turned. He fought less. He wandered more, dirt streets of rodeo towns when the day was done, the lit roads of Bozeman. It was the sound of gravel beneath his boots he sought, a multitude of small stones forming a silver path under the moon and sky, leading nowhere. In summer he rode back through Paradise Valley, then farther south through the great park, where he passed beneath President Roosevelt's grand stone arch below the steam mountains at Mammoth. Above Gardiner he traveled behind the government outbuildings all the way to the headwaters of the Yellowstone at Yellowstone Lake, a wide span of water silver-gray among the dark of high forests. He took the descent north, riding over an open plain under a flare of sun where the white bones of buffalo were still spread like the remnants of dinosaurs.

He emerged again into the kingdom of men at a rodeo in Three Forks. There the confluence of the Gallatin, the Madison, and the Jefferson met to form the Missouri. The rodeos brought solace, the Indian rodeos more than most. He got his nickname Middie early on from riding a crusty rancher's old swaybacked bull when the man taunted him in front of the hands. He'd looked silly riding that bull, and the name stuck. He didn't mind the name Middie.

At Three Forks the water went north nearly all the way to the Highline before bending east, where it joined the Yellowstone and fell south further on, splitting America in two on its way to the Mississippi and the Gulf of Mexico.

Bruised and still burdened, he returned almost full circle to

Bozeman. A great depression on, jobs scarce. He worked on roads, dug ditches, erected train trestles. For a time he got on at Fort Peck for the prebuild on the reservoir, his home a hillside cutout, tarp angled over a woodstove, single three-legged stool, small lamp of oil. He smelled the earth, he slept on dirt. He sold the old woman's horse for five dollars.

South still but jobless again, he waited overnight in a line of one hundred men. The head man saw his size and took him on for labor with the railroad. He'd earn some money, Zion thought, buy himself some land, maybe buy back the land they'd lost. Plant a hedge of wild rose for his mother. He was six feet five inches tall and weighed over two hundred fifty pounds. He worked the North Coast Limited, the interstate rail from east to west. They all called him Middie now. He worked with muscle and grit. He shoveled coal and kept his own peace.

Alone in the late push across the southern line through Montana, he stopped for a moment and rested his hands on the heel of the shovel, his chin on his hands. On his first trip east a workman at the roundhouse in St. Paul threw himself between the cars of an outgoing train. The man was severed in two at the chest. His eyes stared toward heaven, and Middie could not erase the image. He felt the locomotive spending its light toward the oncoming darkness, toward the tiny crossings with unknown names, the towns of eight or ten people. He felt the wide wind, saw the stars in their opaque immensity. A column of smoke churned upward from the head of the locomotive. Among the forests and along the rivers he saw black bears and grizzlies: *Ursus americanus, Ursus arctos horribilis*, names he knew from his learning. He heard the long-nosed scream of the train, bent in the night, and he paused to consider how fully the night fell, how easily the light gave way, before he returned to his work.

He stank of smoke and oil. The sweat of his body enveloped him as he fell toward sleep. In his place in the dark, often he heard his mother. *Mind your schooling,* she said. It was after dinner. He was a child sleeping, and in the silence between night and dawn, waking him, she spoke, pressed her cheek to his small cheek, whispered, *Awake, awake O Zion, clothe yourself in strength. Put on your garments of splendor.* She smoothed his eyebrows with a forefinger. *You can get up now,* she said. She touched his face with her hand.

Black Kettle, 1907

20.

Forty-three years after Sand Creek, William Black Kettle was born to the line of Woman Hereafter, great-great grandson of Black Kettle, the peace chief. Born to Georgie Black Kettle and his wife Luvinia, William was a small child with a piercing cry who grew late but fierce, an agile runner, ken of horses, kin to speed.

William entered the world pink with wet black hair that held some red. When his mother saw his hair, she remembered the Welsh mountain man who had married into the tribe. She also remembered his half-breed son, who had been the interpreter with the whites, a kind redheaded man with a big bear chest and hot eyes whose spirit filled the lodge. The man who married Magpie. William was his name, and the name of his father, and she named her son the same. William Black Kettle. She loved the words as they played in her mouth. She was a strong woman with square shoulders and laughter in her eyes. Her milk smelled sweet. She smiled to see the child hungry, so hungry to get his fill as she lay with her husband in the summer lodge. With the babe in her arms, she held his heel in the palm of her hand, glad for the fullness of life.

FITTED TO THE white man's suits in winter at the one-room thick-chinked cabin that was the Catholic school on the easternmost edge of the reservation, William hardly wore anything in summer. Moccasins his grandmother made, leggings, and the skin of his chest. He loved to run, loved horses, rode horses for speed and leaps and turns, and even as a boy to gather birds, rabbits, and deer to help feed his people. This, north of Lame Deer, generally by snare, or with a gun on occasion when his father let him use the prized .22-caliber Remington Arms single-shot the family kept hidden.

Winters, the People sheltered in the four-walled government houses built by the white man, wooden and square-shaped. Summers, the People returned to their lodges.

Winters, he also studied with the Sisters of God. They taught him to write and read. He grew to love the tasks, for, because of them, the white language became to him beautiful, the language of the People's death, his father told him, the language of their new life. In the years of his schooling he learned to speak both French and English. He wrote exquisitely, growing in his knowledge of word and world. The language in his mouth was stark and eloquent, warrior-like one minute but in the next moment as light-filled as water, and as lovely.

Always the language surprised him with its flexible, sinewy

muscle. Like the body of his people, he thought, though he wasn't foolish. He knew it as the language of the white invaders. He also saw all language, in fact all people, including himself, as capable of not only hate but evil. He learned because he saw language for what it was, a medium through which people granted one another death or life.

The sisters indoctrinated him into the subtle, if profound idea that beauty would save the world. In fact, the Superior had brought two portraits with her from St. Louis, "of the great poets," she smiled wryly, "Christina Rossetti and Elizabeth Barrett Browning." The portraits were black-and-white hand drawings in narrow dark alder-wood frames. They hung in the schoolhouse like spirits and he spent much time studying them, the shape of each woman's nose, the lay of her hair, the barely contained fury that emanated from her eyes.

He cherished those two portraits because they reminded him of the wild he knew in horses and himself. He had a sure affection for horses and rode with an authority that belied his age. His life with his family was different than his life in the schoolhouse.

"WILLIAM," HIS MOTHER called from where she sat beside the lodge, but he'd already leapt to the animal's shoulders, his father's big brown horse. Then he was off over the edge, down through the bed of the coulee and out onto open ground.

"Crazy boy," she whispered. His hair behind him matched the mane of the horse.

Her husband, Georgie, stood beside her. "Let him go," he said. "He finds his way."

She put her cheek to Georgie's leg. She nodded as she turned back to her work with the thumb scraper, cleaning fresh hide while she chewed old leather to soften it for a purse or some gloves. Georgie wore the new ribbon shirt she'd made of purple cloth with faint red ribbons. She admired him with her eyes. He sat down with her.

Many Indian men wore the uniform of the cowboy, domed hats and cuffed work shirts, a neckerchief, pointed boots. She loved to see her husband and son in the clothes she made for them.

"Is he as you thought he'd be?" she asked.

"He is more," he said as he lay down, placing his head on her thigh. He gazed at the rift of land into which young boy and fleet horse had gone and the openness beyond it where the dust rose in small clouds behind the form that moved quickly over the plain.

WILLIAM BLACK KETTLE and Raymond Killsnight were knit together as if before they were born. Their mothers like sisters, the two boys grew closer than brothers.

The boys were thin as cattails along the riverbed but they ran like deer, limber and fast. Joy met their tongues with the new day. They emerged from pools of milky water where the river seemed to walk against itself before they clambered glistening up the far bank. Laughing and shouting, they sped out on open land.

Tough, crafty when they met the pack of older boys, they fought for each other. From a young age they drew others to them and the old men smiled at their exuberance. The old women spoke openly to their mothers. "They'll lead," the women said. "The others will follow." Their mothers cherished what was said about the children, whispering these things to their fathers on the edge of sleep.

Luvinia loved how her husband told stories of the People to his son, stories of the Tsitsistas and their brothers the Suhtai, of peace and goodwill. Stories of the ancient time so long ago when there was no war. She lay with him in the lodge and remembered when he smoothed the ground in front of him and made two marks in the dirt with his right thumb, two with his left, then a double mark with both thumbs together. He rubbed his hand up his right leg to the waist, touched his left hand and passed it up his right arm to his chest. He did the same on the other side. Then he touched the marks on the ground with both hands before he passed his hands over his head, then moved them over his entire body. "The Creator is witness," he said. "*Nih-aahtohvits.* Listen. The father of all Cheyenne horses was blue. The mare was buckskin, and from these every Cheyenne horse was made." He made a fist and stared into William's eyes, saying, "The ones we steal are only coming home."

TRUE ENOUGH, WILLIAM and Raymond would lead the day. When William came into his own the sisters, his teachers, found in him two angels, a firebrand who breathed the fire of God and a servant of peace who brought the People hope. His fire a fire of days and years. His kindness uncommon.

He made them smile. He made them wonder at the ways of heaven.

Above all, he wrote two letters the sisters held dear, both to the Governor of Montana: one when he was not yet thirteen years old but already advanced in their estimation, another when he was seventeen, his voice nearly fully formed.

The first, sent to then Governor Samuel V. Steward, was graced with pathos and precision. "I am your brother," William said. "My people are your children, as your people are mine." He asked the governor to be generous and keep William's people from starving.

To this letter, William Black Kettle received no response.

THE SECOND LETTER he sent four years later, reminding then governor Joseph M. Dixon not only of the Sand Creek Massacre of 1864 but also of the Friendship Treaty of 1825, "a pledge of peace between the Cheyenne and the United States."

"We must make peace again," William declared. "We can live in dignity, as friends who respect and care for each other. I am neither your slave nor your enemy. I am your fellow man."

Some ten months later William received an ignominious reply. In fact, the governor never saw the letter. The reply came from correspondence staffer James Whitaker, who said, simply, "Do not expect the spoils of the conqueror."

1924

21.

SHOT FROM THE chute like a bird wide open, like a hawk through a gap of wind and stone, the horse coiled before it sprang forth, carrying him as if the animal bore wings. The calf ahead seemed to pause in midflight, snot from the nose and head lunging forward. William rose in the saddle as he circled the rope overhead, smooth in the wrist, quick on the turn. The release came like laying a loved one down, like a braid of sweet-grass in the hand. Eyes, arms, and chest in perfect confluence, he lofted the rope over the calf's head as he set the horse's hooves on a back lean. He leapt to the ground following the taut rope as the horse cut the dirt, the calf tilting on a line upward with William close enough to catch it in midair. Hand in glove, rope in hand, dirt in mouth, teeth and tongue, he riled up dust over the grounds like smoke. He took the slack over the calf hip, flipped the animal shoulder to bone, straddling it as he snatched the piggin string from his mouth, wrapping the front hoof and tying the two back hooves in a flourish. Hands free, chest out in a loud whoop, he let his hat fly while he walked with his head up, smiling all the way back to the horse. The crowd applauded his work. Earlier Raymond had won in steer jerking. Now William was a sure winner in calf roping.

William let his face come placid while he trotted his horse out of the arena back to the staging area where he gave the horse water and let the horse eat.

This horse he'd chosen personally from the Cheyenne herd of fifteen thousand. A true cutting horse, a warhorse, part quarter horse with mustang and Spanish blood, a black-and-white paint firm in the haunches, tall at the shoulder, intelligent, and with great heart. Good shoulder slope, natural angle to the neck. Fast to the rope. This horse carried him and made him fly.

BACK HOME, WILLIAM'S father and mother bore the injury of enemies and generations. He wanted to please them, and lift their spirits. He felled deer, elk and antelope. He excelled at arrow throwing and hand games. He played hoop games and stick games at Cheyenne Fair. Of a gentle spirit, he broke horses well. He rode fast among the coulees, encountering strange rock formations where the bodies of old Cheyenne warriors were laid to rest upon shelves of sandstone. He walked his horse among them. Eying the bones, he remembered the old ones, their stories around the fires.

His face grew dark when he thought of Sand Creek. If he let himself dwell, the result was that he wanted only to take up the hammer and ax. But remembering his father's eyes brought him back. This was how he learned to be at peace. A warrior, yes, a soldier chief, perhaps, but like his father, and his father's fathers, he hoped he would one day be a peace chief. The People needed peace chiefs, he thought, or they would be destroyed. He would be what his father desired him to be, a path from this world to the white world.

In the night William's mother sang to him her healing song, her song for the new day. The song of Sweet Medicine from her lips, like willow and wind, the song from Woman Hereafter to William from before he was born.

WILLIAM HAD LIVED in a pledge tipi now for one year, alone for purification. Tomorrow he would perform a healing ceremony for the descendants of the Sand Creek Massacre, men and women come to make peace over the dead. He removed the pipe from its leather wrapping. A pipe made of good red stone that his uncle Edwin Black Kettle had held for the family before he'd gone missing when William was a boy.

"The pipe is for you," his uncle had said. "For when you are older. *Naytahahoh-na*. May Maheo direct you when and where to use it."

WILLIAM SAT BEFORE the center fire. It was night, and he had completed his pledge only four days before. He was full grown, and the People looked to him as he prepared to make his first Sun Dance. With him, Georgie and Luvinia would perform a healing ceremony for the People. Raymond would join him.

Both young men pledged the New Life Lodge for the healing of the Tsitsistas, the Cheyenne.

The circle of tipis rose around William, and he felt strong seated next to his father. Wolverine, his animal, moved across mountain ranges in the dark, finding his way still to his sons and daughters, his children who roamed the earth and played on the high places.

The next day William went to the mountain early to see the Morning Star come. He gave thanks, and made his return down the mountain. Over the plain a swift hawk flew, big, blue-toned with black stripes across the tail feathers. He thought of Brave Wolf, who the elders said rode into battle blowing a bone whistle, a mounted swift hawk tied to the back lock of his hair. The old ones said Brave Wolf licked the tail feathers of the hawk and tasted the sky. Today the bird flew high and fast. Far below the bird the hoods of a few Model Ts from the Bureau of Indian Affairs men flashed like turtle shells, black in the sun. Horse carriages made up the circumference. Men on horseback looked on.

William began to run, surefooted and nearly silent in the morning. His heart leapt to see the tipis set in wide concentric circles down below the horse carriages where the river arced west. As he drew close, he smelled the scent of woodsmoke and sage. He brought his hands to his face and smelled the sweetgrass he carried. He yelled and some of those who walked near the Sun Dance Lodge lifted their heads and yelled back to him, smiling to see him run.

Dancers from the north and from the south converged for the round dance. The songs reminded him of wolves and of Coyote. The drum sounded like big weather on the mountain.

He walked through a field where dun grasshoppers startled, flying like members of a tribe of dust. The click-clack sound of their black-and-yellow wings accompanied him. The sun was full over the land.

The rich scent of buffalo and fry bread. The feast roasted in the fire pit, and as the dancers danced William prepared himself. He walked among his people to the center of camp, where the altar of the buffalo skull was painted with earth, the eyes and nose stuffed with grasses.

The People entered the Sun Dance Lodge. Outside, others gave witness. Some were draped in white cloth that blanketed body and limbs, hiding the hands, the cloth a covering for the head and face, showing only the eyes. William looked into their eyes as he passed.

William sat down in the circle, his father beside him, his mother behind his left shoulder. The coat of a badger lay in his father's lap, stretched and dried. Prepared by his mother long ago. The fringe was lined with beaded design, the long, black-tipped tails of the weasel, and the blue jay's bright-feathered fan. Raymond and his father, Bull, the war chief, sat to William's right. William lifted the sacred pipe, holding it with both hands on the stem as his father had taught him.

In a loud voice his father said, "Let us remember Sand Creek together. Women and children dead. Bodies desecrated and the parts taken for show in the white cities. Nearly two hundred dead even after Black Kettle the chief raised the American flag and the white flag of peace.

"Defenseless."

He paused. "And let us also remember the Fetterman fight two years after Sand Creek, when Cheyenne and Sioux led eighty-one government soldiers into an ambush and killed the soldiers in a rain of arrows that left no one alive. Women and men, the ones who had relatives killed at Sand Creek, came out and chopped off the heads and arms. They took what they wanted. Coats and caps, gloves, weapons, boots.

"And let us remember the Cheyenne scouts who served with the white cavalry officers for two decades at the end of the Indian Wars. After they were discharged, some of them wore their uniforms at dances and celebrations until they passed to the next life. They were proud of those uniforms.

"Let us remember our history, a history we share, Indian and white.

"Today is a good day to forgive. We give thanks to Maheo."

22.

IN TONGUE RIVER country in early summer with the grass high so the game was plentiful, warriors from five societies rode hard over the plain. The men went down through coulees and up draws until the interweaving of horse and men became like braids on the back of the earth.

There the land was tanned like the inside of a buffalo hide and open from the sun's rise to its descent. The gossamer of warm weather, the long shadow of summer. In among willows, whitetop, and star thistle, the river went forth bearing the sun so that the color of water changed like the land, silver-gold and subdued to blue, then gray, then black again toward night.

In the night, fires.

The Cheyenne camp encircled itself, horses bedded in the fields beyond, the sound of whistles, drum, and laughter musical in the blackness. The bands had gathered in a great circle opening to the east. The wind smelled of animal fat.

William's father, Georgie, walked into the New Life Lodge again, remembering his brother Edwin, gone these many years. He gave thanks to the Great Spirit for his father and mother and all his relations. His mother, Bird in Ground, stood near the entrance of the lodge. The old Chief American Horse stood near her, still brawny even after all he'd endured. A vision came to Georgie of Two Childs, the great medicine man from Highwalker's band who had died so well. Georgie took courage. Two Childs's power came from the buffalo. He wore a buffalo tail tied to the back lock of his hair.

THE DANCERS WERE all seated now. To their left were two elders, Elmer Coal Bear and Hester Walks Nice, priests. They kept the medicine bundles for the good of the People, the buffalo hat Esevone and the arrow bundle Mohuts, the sacred symbols of woman and man. William rose as the elders directed him, taking the sweetgrass in his hands as he passed among the men in the circle and knelt before them. He wafted smoke over their bodies and up into their faces. Luvinia's eagle fan moved among them, a fan from Georgie's mother.

The pipe was filled with tamped kinnikinnick and tobacco, sweetgrass incense placed on top, and passed around the circle. In the center of the circle the pipe was lifted to the four directions.

The pipe moved from man to man. The men took two or three puffs. Some were silent. Some gave a blessing. "From Maheo. New life," an older man said. William spoke. "We seek peace. Sons and daughters of the Cheyenne. We ask Maheo to heal our tears." To his right Raymond's father, Bull, had his chin on his chest, eyes closed, torment etched on his face.

"Today we forgive," said William's father. "Today the dancers honor the reconciliation ceremony."

Horses moved along the perimeter, riderless. They bore the star blankets of the Cheyenne, blankets to be given as gifts to the elders.

In the touch of the hand, remembrance. In the voice, tenderness.

"*Hay eheh, eh pehvah*. It is good," William's father said. He held the pipe of peace high.

23.

THE CENTER POLE rose above the place of prayer. Cottonwood limbs shorn from a river tree, thick-leaved and ripe with life, were set near the entrance, over the buffalo skull. Long full-growth limbs, dark green at dusk, flickering yellow underlit by fire, were leaned against the center pole. Here William and Raymond danced, their bodies painted white. They wore loincloths and long leggings. Their painters painted red lines on them from forehead to hipline, like narrow streams of blood down the face to the body, down the arms, down the chest to the waist. Their hands too were dark with red paint. There is life, William thought, there shall be new life.

William had come to the New Life Lodge fasting. He and Raymond had watched their friends eat and asked Maheo for generosity for the People. The two of them danced near one another into the deep dark, the starlight of Quillwork Girl and the

Seven Brothers up through the open center of the lodge like tips of spears in the night, the light holding up the dark.

As William danced the moon rose. Here when his mouth tasted of dust while his fists stood woven with grasses, William sensed the coming of the sun far off like a child awaits his father. William felt hot tears on his face, mixed with the blood-paint and the white base. He was drawn facedown to the earth near the center pole, where he closed his eyes and wept until he slept.

In the day, strange dreams. Outside the lodge a deserted land filled with sandrock cliffs and scattered jack pine, no brush, no timber. The mouths of crickets sang out. He felt the earth alive with insects and anthills.

That night he danced again. And the next night.

In the new world of the third dawn it seemed he stood still but the rhythm of his body still moved. He was asleep and not asleep, alive and half dead. He saw himself as from a distance, the bones buried in his chest attached with rawhide ropes stiff and taut to the apex of the lodge. The piercing seemed so long ago. Now with his arms and head slung back, his hair full over his back, he swayed, suffering, until at last a great pressure seemed to pull him down as if from below the earth, a force that snatched at his upper body as he shook on the bone wires until his body collapsed beneath him.

Someone placed a buffalo robe over him. They cut away the strings of flesh from his chest, leaving a clean wound. He bled. He slept.

As one in the house of the dead. As one who wakes to new life.

24.

WILLIAM AND RAYMOND took to the road early. They wore the buckskins their mothers had made for them, keeping to more covered terrain. They rode much at night to avoid alarming the whites. They were sent forth by the People to rodeos near and far in order to make a name for themselves and the Cheyenne. They camped in the lee of swales or at the base of stone outcroppings or among trees. They drank from streams and rivers. The rivers they crossed quickly on the white man's bridges, the Tongue, then the Yellowstone, the Poplar, the Missouri, and from there to points north or west. They took blankets and buffalo hides, enough jerked beef for the journey. They concealed their fathers' old rifles. In their bedrolls they stored the tribe's gifts for the dignitaries they met—beaded moccasins, gloves, leggings, vests, and pipe bags. They also carried their finest white man's clothes: denim pants and wool vests, white shirts they washed in river water.

Once they returned south, crossing the Montana line into Cheyenne, Wyoming to rope at Frontier Days, and it was here they met the giant, a huge white bulldogger who called himself Middie.

Just before William and Raymond won the team roping handily, the big man finished a tough steer in four seconds, a mean animal marbled and tow-horned. William watched from the fence as the man rode a powerful horse, bent himself, and launched onto the steer's back, riding it down as he turned the head light and quick. The steer went hooves up. The crowd hollered and lost their hats. Like the legend of Bill Pickett, William thought, only chalk-white.

After the rodeo William walked a field near Crow Creek on the outer ring of the rodeo grounds. His horse fed as he waited for Raymond who'd gone to seek more tobacco. The creek was clear over smooth stones. The wimple and whirl of brook trout met the current.

He saw the giant on the far northern edge of the rodeo grounds. The man waved once and walked his horse toward William. From that distance the bones and the height of the man made a bear-like vision. He approached directly, and at first William balled his fists, unsure if the man might want to fight. But the big man let his horse drift. Lifting his hands in friendship, he said, "Admired your work today."

"Thank you," William said. "Same to you with the bulldogging."

"Cheyenne?" the big man ventured.

"Yes," William said, a hint of a grin on his face. "You too?"

"White as white," Middie said, and they laughed together.

"How'd you make out I'm Cheyenne?" William asked.

"Smile a good deal," Middie said. "I rode with some over the years. Your people what the old cavalry officers called the Beautiful People." They sat down then in a matter-of-fact-way in the short white grass on the bank that overlooked over the creek.

"Where are your people from," he said, "Lame Deer?"

"Tongue River country north," said William, "over St. X and Busby way. Yours?"

"On the Highline near Canada," the big man said. "Before that from Europe, on accord of my momma's kin. Germany. Place she called Wolfenbuttel. All dead now.

"Mighty fine roping today," he said again, nodding his head in approval.

The water moved east, thin-bodied and clean as glass until it rippled to small white crests at the bend.

"William Black Kettle," William said, putting his hand out.

"Middie," the big man said, firmly shaking William's hand. "Pleased to make your acquaintance."

The country swept out flat to the horizon south and west, needle grass with tumbleweed on the air. In the distance the Laramie Range was steady to the sky. The final day before the trek onward to more rodeos. William and Raymond had made quick work. They'd leave in the morning before the heavy drinking began in town. Middie likely did not fear towns, William thought.

The sun still high on the descent, their horses nosed near each other, Middie's great sorrel a giant in its own right, blond in the mane and tail, alongside William's black-and-white paint, lean and sure-footed, a few hands shorter than Middie's horse.

They talked about rodeos and events, rides, spills, the best way to use a fire for setting the juice in the meat, fry bread, choke-cherry patties, pemmican, potatoes in a broth of sauce and bird meat. Fights, animals, wilderness. They spoke of where they'd been and where they planned to go. In the end Middie asked William about his family, and William related stories of dance and celebration, songs, the work to keep everyone fed. Middie watched the creek, thinking of his mother. He felt more than a little sorrow.

"Where's the Cheyenne who heels for you?" Middie said.

"Tobacco," William said and motioned with his lips toward town. Dark was coming on. "Raymond Killsnight's his name. Like a brother to me. Share our fire tonight if it suits you."

"Obliged," said Middie, and when Raymond returned the three had a meal of young pronghorn Middie shot a short ride out, along with small red potatoes and the tin of butter Middie had picked up in town earlier before placing it in the creek to cool. They lay back and rested their feet on the ground as they slanted their heads to their hands. They laughed plenty and slept soundly.

In the morning they ate from the jerked deer and peppered bacon Raymond carried, drinking it down with hard coffee. They watched a skein of sandhill crane glide the stream on a path south.

After they parted William thought long of the encounter. Middie was a white man who spoke easily with Indians. Raymond took to him as much as William. Going their separate ways, they had shaken hands after promising to share another meal the next time they met.

THE RODEOS WENT on mostly in the white towns, where alcohol and gambling went hand in glove, with a small few on the reservations, where there was less prize money but a victory brought stunning beadwork. William and Raymond never again found the kind of ease with another white person they had found with the giant. But the giant they saw more than once, and they smiled to see him. Sitting together over bacon or stew on the Highline near Froid or farther west at Fort Belknap or Great Falls, a kinship came to them.

In towns like Broadus, south near the Dakota border, or east to Hardin and Billings, each time the Cheyenne took a white man's money at rodeo it resulted in a sharp-edged thrill, but the money was sometimes hard to keep. They were beaten up twice when they let themselves get cornered—simple unthinking decisions, riding through town rather than skirting it, finding themselves blacked out in the dirt before they rose to lift their bodies back home. Lucky they weren't killed. But they'd delivered their own beatings too: when a drunk farmer behind the Stockman in Billings drew a knife, William punched the butt of his rifle in the man's face. On the edge of the rodeo grounds in Roundup Raymond broke a wooden cattle prod over the back of a slim cowboy's head. In both cases they ran the horses hard away from the white settlements before the lynching began.

EVELYNNE LOWRY, 1926

25.

THREE YEARS AFTER Tomás's death, Evelynne's horse, Chloe, fell ill and died. She had not ridden the horse since that day in the canyon when she'd seen Tomás steeped in dust. The sting of her horse's passing caused a second collapse in her, a landslide into a larger pain within the small hermitage of solitude that was her bedroom at the ranch house. Death follows death, she thought. She often felt ghostly descending the stairs to where she crossed the threshold through the front doors out into the open field. What are we, she thought, but here and gone?

Walking in fog through a windless field, she stared at the mountain and paced forward into the trees. She knew pain at the memory of a certain scripture: *Our days are like grass. We flourish like a flower in the field, but the wind blows over it and the flower is gone, and its place remembers it no more.* But we are remembered, she told herself, arguing with God. She wouldn't allow the possibility of anyone she loved ever being forgotten. People fall to the earth, and here we are remembered no more. But we ascend, where we are known forever. She thought of how darkness holds fire. How fire moves to greater fire. Her heart welled with sadness. "Yes," she whispered. Both the infinite and oblivion require release.

At her bravest, she followed paths she had often taken with her horse and returned to her room feeling raw and forsaken. She questioned how she could have done what she'd done. Taken her brother north. Left the horse so alone. She carried small stones with her like a penance in summer, and in winter she walked until her fingers were nearly frostbitten before she came back to the house to stare into the fire. Finally she stayed inside and went out only on rare occasions. The cadence of poetry remained, her thoughts adrift in the white between the lines. In the evening her father came to her when she beckoned to read long passages of Milton and Browning until she slept.

Upon taking his leave he kissed her forehead. "Child," he said over her, "come back to us, come back to me." There was a tenderness in him she had not fully acknowledged.

She begged him, be he drunk or sober, to speak to her of Tomás, and always he refused. "Don't test me," he said. If she pressed, his tone became sharp. The grief hurts him, she thought, more than he knows. Finally, in regret over her horse's passing and with spite over her father's silence regarding Tomás, she holed up in her room, choosing not to emerge. Her father arranged for her meals to be delivered to her, but he did not approve of this turn of events. He could not bear to watch her become a recluse.

Daily he went to the city on business and kept his war room active. On occasion he would need to be gone weeks at a time, to D.C. or New York City. He sent Chan to her then, but when home Josef returned to the ranch house, where at day's end he attended her, speaking with kindness in his voice. In her poems, as if in response to his generosity, she began slowly to make a return, and when she commenced setting them again on the standing table outside her door, he took them to the great room where he smiled at the slant of her handwriting, fluid and, as ever, open like her mother's. The lay of the words in their dignity gave him pause.

Her poems accumulated, and when they came more constant, at some few per month, he let them gather, at last choosing what he thought to be the best among them before he sent three in her name to the *Atlantic Monthly* in Boston. The return post was long in coming, but at last a letter of fine distinction arrived from editor Ellery Sedgwick, stating, "Miss Lowry, I find your verses delightful. Your heart for man is not only necessary, but ebullient. I'm pleased to publish these important poems you sent. Please send more at your leisure. I shall receive them with gratitude."

When Josef gave his daughter the letter, the absolute clarity in her eyes was the first he'd witnessed since the death of her brother. Thus began a correspondence between her and Mr. Sedgwick that resulted in her first full-length book of poems read by a national audience. Through Sedgwick's influence the book spread by good fortune to Paris and London, from which, along with disparate points throughout America, she received earnest letters of admiration from both women and men. The women plumbed unforeseen depths in her words. The men expressed unabashed sympathy and not a few proposals of marriage.

Still she kept to her room and refused to go outside.

Regarding men, her father simply said, "No," and she nodded. She couldn't imagine herself in another house.

Only Chan's visits brought word of the outside world. He came cloaked in black with a black bowler he placed on the floor beside him as he drew up a simple wooden armchair and spoke without stop sometimes for an hour or more. Always he presented his knowledge balanced and rational as if, though she herself felt burdened, life were only a collection of decisions that resulted in what men called fate. History came from his mouth like water from a deep well. The old agony at Death Valley, the starvation in the mines of Forlorn Hope, the abundance in the mountains of Montana, silver and gold, yes, but more immanent the immense veins of copper. He spoke of vast herds of cattle, along with vigilantes in the shadow of the great Sioux and Cheyenne uprisings, the recent lie of railroads to all points north, south, east, and west. The deep rock cuts through which trains passed like steel camels through the eye of a needle. The Chinese workers, his brothers, he called them, the old-time one-horse dump carts they used, the great wooden trestles and the fires, entire swaths of city lost to fire, New York and Chicago, Seattle, San Francisco. From of old, he told of General William T. Sherman and Brigham Young, Red Cloud and Spotted Tail. This he paired with the modern day. The intricate webs of electricity carried by networks of copper through the great cities, and how such copper came from right here on the big hill in Butte.

She loved to hear him speak and nearly forgot her isolation.

All was calmer now, he said, after the Great War. He sat with his hands on his thighs, a sparkle in his eyes. Though she allowed herself her own vanities—the dresses she donned each day for the writing table, the felt hat and gloves she set atop the bureau by the door—she remained in her room, not venturing out. In this way she granted herself the dignity of a living devotion, yet without having to face the world of men.

Alone, I do no harm, she thought. Chan's voice was a comfort. She would affirm love in her own solitary way. Love, she thought, imprints us with courage. When she wrote she preferred her skirts fluted or bustled, capped by corsets and fitted coats, all character-istically Victorian and of a darker palette. She cared not a whit if they were no longer in style. In the mirror the cut made her shoul-ders and bust traditionally elegant, with a clean, fetching waistline. She favored this over the ill-fitting sacks in vogue in the catalogs her father brought from the east. Despite the near disappearance of the bustle from the department stores of Chicago and New York he had her garments tailored as she directed.

Her father feared her seclusion but liked that she was not so headstrong and wild now. She responded to each letter she re-ceived. In the women she recognized a true kinship and solidar-ity whose varied paths the world over seemed to converge in antiwar sentiment along with a kind of intrepid stewardship for the plight of unfortunates. With the men, those few who kept on, she was forthright, speaking with discretion, always passing her letters before her father. To those who asked for her hand, she wrote once but not again, declaring to them unequivocally her singular unavailability.

BLACK KETTLE

26.

AFTER THE SUN dance, after William and Raymond suffered, and now that they rodeoed and roped together, everyone could see that the spirit of Raymond was woven to the spirit of William. Raymond gave his prized buffalo robe to William with his grandfather's elk-bone breastplate, along with a very good hunting knife, sheath and belt. William gave Raymond a beautiful elk-bone choker his mother made as well as an elk-tooth shirt of his grandfather's that was the pride of the clan. He also asked his father to give him a fine young horse to give to Raymond.

"I'll be a brother to you always," William said.

"As I am your brother." Raymond responded, and they embraced one another like men.

BUT SOON THE face of Raymond's father darkened toward William.

Bull Killsnight was a fearsome chief, not inclined to white men's ways. Each winter Bull helped supply the People with fur. He found river otter, beaver, red fox, fisher, coyote, wolf, and mink, all in his snare traps along the river and up in the wooded places.

Bull would not be passive. He led the People. When he saw his son and William shoulder to shoulder in the light of day, he knew the People favored William over Raymond, and his heart grew remote. The People's talk of William leading, Raymond following, displeased him. "They place my son behind Black Kettle," said Bull.

And William felt his malintent.

Of an evening in autumn, when Raymond was away hunting in the hills, a distressing spirit came over Bull Killsnight. He went brooding until he found William singing by the center fire. Bull went directly to his own lodge, took up his stone hammer, and returned to the fire. The leather handle felt good in his hand. He raised his arm and threw the hammer at William. William heard the wind of it sift the hair above his ear before the weapon glanced off the top of his shoulder.

The bruise was deep but not fatal. William looked at Bull and bowed his head. Bull walked away, disappearing into his lodge. The People went silent.

WILLIAM RODE TO find Raymond then. He drew his friend away to the river, where they stood in blue willows at the water's edge. "What have I done?" William said. "Why does your father want me dead?"

And Raymond said, "No, he does not want you dead! You will not die! My father tells me his heart. Why would he hide this?"

"Your father sees we're brothers now," William said, "but Maheo gives life, and as your spirit lives, your father wants to kill me."

Raymond bit the inside of his cheek, tasting blood in his mouth. "Whatever you desire, William," he said, "I'm ready."

So William said, "Tomorrow is the new moon. Your father will expect me at the feast and dancing. But I'll hide in the coulees south along the river. If your father misses me, then tell him, 'William has gone to gather more game. He'll return to the dance when the moon rises.' If your father says, 'Good, I'm glad,' it will go well for me, but if he is angered, then know he intends to harm me. If it is so, be kind to me if you find me as a brother still. But if I have wronged you or your family, kill me yourself."

And Raymond said, "Never! We are brothers. Have we not always been so? If he means to harm you, I'll tell you."

Raymond continued, "Tonight during the feast I'll come to you. Hide among these big trees." His hands gestured to a stand of cottonwoods among chokecherry and ash. "Once I've looked into my father's intentions, I'll come to the cut bank there above the trees." He pointed to a high bank into which the river moved before taking the curve and descending again like muddy milk farther south. "If he is happy with you, then all is well. But if he wants to kill you, then you must flee. As for us, Maheo binds me to you forever. I'll never undo our vow."

So William returned to camp, gathering his belongings, and traveled a mile downriver, where he hobbled the horse at the forelegs so it could feed unnoticed. Then William hid himself among the trees below camp.

When evening fell, the dance began. Bull Killsnight came from his lodge and stood off on the edge of the center circle in the shadows. He held a heavy-headed spear to his side.

Raymond approached his father. "Will you come to the round dance?" he said. "You are a chief, it's good for the People that we dance together."

"Where's William?" Bull said.

"He went to gather more food for the feast," said Raymond.

Then Bull's hatred kindled, rising against his own Raymond. He turned to his son, saying, "Son of a whore! To your shame you choose him over yourself. As long as William lives, you will be less. He'll be more. Go. Bring him to me so I can kill him."

Raymond answered his father, "Why should he die? What has he done?"

Hearing his son answer this way, Bull Killsnight struck Raymond across the neck with the blunt face of the spear, knocking him to the ground. Raymond rose and looked fiercely at his father before retreating into the forest. He circled the camp, the fire ablaze from the center of the round dance. With sorrow he paused at a crease in the lodge stands where he saw the People in their slow march around the fire. The scent of cooked deer meat came to him. His father stood on the far edge of the flames, his face held by the play of shadow and light, his eyes sunken in darkness.

Raymond rode quickly to the cut bank, where he whistled the song of the mountain bluebird. William rose from cover, and

Raymond dismounted, running around the lip of the cut bank to the ground along the riverbed, where they stood face to face. "Fly to the hills," Raymond said. "My father seeks to kill you." They put their heads together and wept, Raymond weeping the most.

IN THE COMING days the people wondered about William's absence. William's father sought Raymond, who told him what had happened. Georgie and Luvinia Black Kettle were grieved but kept silent, awaiting the fate of Maheo. Word spread among the People, causing them to give Bull Killsnight a wide berth. No one could reason with him or even speak William's name without awakening the bear in him.

Raymond sought William in the hills with no word but to wait.

Bull Killsnight's fury was unabated.

William lived on his own in the land on the edge of the tribe, making his home among the winding paths where sandstone bled to sage. The ground held tufts of grass that bent in the wind and he wondered what the elders might decide about the distance Bull Killsnight had placed between him and the People. He ate deer and rabbit, chokecherries, and on occasion black medicine or bitterroot with a little sugar brought to him by his mother. "*Moh ohtaha heseheoh ohtseh,*" she said. "Good for your spirit." She had no news. No one did, not even Raymond, who stole away on occasion to bring him jerked beef or salt, a little laughter and goodwill.

But before the New Moon feast had passed a year's cycle, he saw his father south along the Tongue, walking slowly toward him on the riverbank. William came near as Georgie reported that Bull Killsnight was dead, killed by a white man near Broadus over a dispute involving cattle.

ZION

27.

AFTER A YEAR of train duty the bosses paid Middie a week's severance for his good work and let him go. With money hard to come by, he fought and made some little cash working as a hand on two ranches half across the state from one another. Two winters passed. No long-term jobs and nearly no silver to be had. He heard of men who took leave of Montana entirely to work on the Tennessee Valley Authority and points east. He lived on deer and antelope, grouse, pheasant, and sage hens, a turkey on occasion when he came upon a gaggle north of Big Timber or down in the cottonwoods near Absarokee below the Beartooths. But it was hard even to keep the Winchester in bullets, he chided himself.

What jobs he found he was grateful for. Day work on occasion, a few weeks' work breaking horses. Rare enough, but he was sometimes lucky. The luck came from his mother, he thought. She'd be praying for him, as he prayed for her. He thought for certain she would call it grace, not luck. He pictured her as she returned from the creekbed, the wooden bucket sloshing water on her shins as she walked. When he was a child, she'd call to him, "Help me, boy," and he'd leave his work and go to her, carrying the bucket in his arms like a basket. She walked beside him. Smiling, she sang quietly to herself. In his memory a thrush followed her as it lit in the crowns of the brush along the creek, the tiny bird yellow-breasted with a black necklace and a black cap. When they arrived at the house, she opened the door to let him pass through before she followed him inside.

He prayed at night before he slept for God to bring him nearer to her, to give her blessed rest. He knew himself to be lonely. He didn't like it, but such was his way. It hadn't been different since he could remember.

Now men knew him not just for wrestling steers but for how well he broke horses. The skill he'd learned from his uncle. "Thorough good work," the men said. "Horse comes out strong, gentle to the rein." He traveled as the road went, east to Billings, where the Northern Cheyenne and the Crow riders roped like their fists were magic, where he saw William and Raymond again before he went north to Wolf Point and west to Browning. Back through the middle of the state, he stopped at Miles City for the Powder River Roundup, where the ranchers and their wives whooped when he rode, as enamored of him and his size as they were of any of the rough stock. Miles City, horse capital of the world, where ranchers ran herds with anywhere from two thousand to ten thousand head of horses. The Dunning ranch by Ashland and the big operation over Coalwood way. They raised Cleveland bays and French coach and draft horses and pretty much every kind of horse you could name. Most, especially about 1912 and after, they had sold to the army, and until the war was over those animals had gone out as packhorses or warhorses. What they sold was range stock: part Indian, part thoroughbred and cavalry remounts, part Texas cow pony. It had been lucrative business in its day. A mix of animals, for certain, he thought, many of them big and wild, with buck in the heart and kick in the leg.

He lost himself to bulldogging and fighting. Steers were a different animal, rangy, with horns nearly a foot long. He loved his horse's strength and speed, loved the lean and leap, his rib cage to the animal's spine as he landed hard on the steer, hands gripping the horns. He lodged the far horn in the crook of his elbow and locked it to his side as he dug his heels into the dirt. He took the muzzle and twisted the jaw head over neck, throwing his weight backward until the steer flipped neat as bacon. When he stood and raised a hand, the crowd applauded.

He fought more than he wanted to as he went from town to town. Wandering, his mother's softly measured words remained a compass to him. *O Zion, put on your garments of splendor.* Though his head was heavy and heart downtrodden, he said the words slowly over and again. To him, America was a fortress of reticence and resolve. His uncle had passed. His father had also fallen, but bitterly. He'd make it, he thought, he wouldn't sell ghost before his time.

28.

AN EMPTINESS IN him he could not be rid of, Middie went forth and bludgeoned the men who challenged him and was sometimes bludgeoned by the steers he challenged. When the day was done he lay on his bedroll in summer, or in the tenement shacks of small towns in winter. Thoughts of death accompanied him often. North across the Highline the rippled flash of the aurora borealis made him wonder at the nature of God and men. When he dove onto a large white brute of a steer at the Indian rodeo in Poplar, the animal pierced his side and nearly accordioned his spine. Three Sioux bullfighters, a Cree, and an Assiniboine were needed to drag him to where he lay in the shade of a tree. The rodeo doctor took a brief look and said he'd be fine. But Middie didn't agree. Toward evening, feeling worse, he gathered himself and mounted his horse.

He went back west along the Highline in a fever of days, hearing the bloodcurdling anthem of coyotes in the night. Massive herds of wild horses roamed the land, and he saw the black vein of their number out over the steppes in the darkness. In daylight he passed a man on horseback with a long dog greyhound and two wolfhound runners, big and lank, their narrow faces muted by eyes that sought the terrain and ran closemouthed until the long dog overtook a lone wolf or coyote and brought the animal down, the two running dogs following to make the kill.

Half a morning further he saw a small barn around Sunburst near Marias Pass. Coyote pelts and wolf skins were tacked to the wood by the nose. The furs covered the entire surface of the south-facing wall, even to the tip of the arch. He sat astride his horse, holding his side. He looked at the barn a long time before he clicked his tongue and moved south. At last, at the edge of consciousness he made his way into the hills, where he entered the mouth of a cave above the bluffs outside Heart Butte.

Here an old Blackfeet woman watched him pass through the opening. She had been out gathering bulbs when she heard the step of the horse and looked up to see him in the distance. She saw how he held himself hunched over with his arms wrapped at his middle. She came to him the next morning and touched his shoulder where he lay, making sure his eyes opened before she left again. When she returned she brought him some jerked deer meat, which she chewed first to soften, an old potato, and water from a leather flask. The food smelled like earth. He'd be dead without her, he thought, and contemplated his will to live, where it came from, and who shepherds the living and the dead.

Winter set in like the teeth of a badger.

His life seemed to walk away from him. He saw the old woman's ancient loose-skinned face in his dreams and woke to her crouched over his chest, her fingers on his lips. Months passed. He fell far into darkness and did not return until the air took on warmth as the land burnished itself again to green and gold. The sound of birdsong a clarion in his ears, meadowlark and pine grosbeak, Steller's jay and black-capped chickadee. The strength slowly returned to his fists and legs. At last his whole body rose up. He went outside, where he found his horse eating from a thatch of fresh hay a short distance below the cave.

Before he left he tracked the old woman's steps to a small village where tipis clung to the north edge of the reservation at a bend in the creek the people there called Bone Whistle. He sat astride his horse and looked down from a low ridge.

From his place among aspen and some few tamarack he saw her far below as she entered through the opening of one of the dwellings. He made note and took the snare traps from his saddlebag. He set the line near a game trail, slept a final night in the cave, and woke early. When he inspected the line he found a marten, two lynx, and a bobcat. To these he added a deer he managed to shoot. He also took two magpies for their ceremonial feathers and came to her with the deer laid over the haunches of his horse, the marten and cats along with the birds hung by hay twine from the pommel horn.

Middie was welcomed by the old woman. He presented his gifts as her people gathered around, watching him kiss her cheek. He cut the buttons off his coat, placing them in her hands while he removed his vest and neckerchief to put them on her. Directly she went into the lodge. Returning, she placed a large wolf skin over his shoulders. She wrapped the tail at his neck while others touched his hair and beard. There was a feast then, with dancing.

He thought he might stay, but in the dark he slipped away while the fires were still high. Under the track of stars he went farther west to the Flathead River, where a great blue heron stood in the shallows nearby. Wide moon overhead, a sky almost as light as day, the gray shawl of the heron's first feathers made a line against the blue of the broad feathers. The heron lifted, beating the air loudly before it glided along the river at a speed that carried it wide around a bend of water. The bird grew smaller and smaller before being wholly lost to view. In the coming days Middie rode along the vast body of Flathead Lake all the way to Wild Horse Island. Finally he chose an angle that led him south along the Mission Range.

Near Ronan he broke horses for the Salish, then made his way toward Missoula, where he hoped he might find more work. Through huge river valleys that took more than a day's ride to cross he rode beneath canopies of cloud and cloud towers, uprisen columns of white like strongholds in the sky. Great swaths of cobalt met his eye. Shafts of sunlight slanted like the hand of heaven touched to earth.

Toward Butte a single bald eagle plied the air along the Clark Fork River.

II.

Footfalls of the horse thud and bump on a pine-needle bed. Slender trees point skyward where limbs mingle with night. The rider's face is white and sharp. Her dark hair glints red against the black of her coat. She carries her hope in her hands and goes where she goes.

Evelynne Lowry, 1928

29.

FIVE YEARS FROM the death of her brother, when at last Evelynne took the carriage to the meadow above the ranch house, her father's eyes filled with tears. Like the mercy of spring, she held desires long foreign to her, to be among people again in the land of the living. Her father rode on the bench beside her, Chan seated on the other side.

Chan made sure she wore her gloves. As she peered out at him, she thought of the care he'd taken to have her wrapped in two coats and a long scarf, a hat of white wool, and an Indian blanket. He watched her face with great consideration.

When she stepped out that first day, after so long behind walls, dawn had arrived and the colors of autumn placed a deep burden on the mountainside. She took her father's arm as she came down beside him. They walked this way twice weekly for half a year before she was first seen in town again.

In late summer she attended a rodeo with her father. Chan,

with an entourage of Chinese as a buffer, walked with her all the way up into the grandstand. Onlookers gawked like fools until at last she was seated, surrounded by her attendants. She in her wine-colored dress like a dab of blood in an inkwell of black, the cloaks and trousers and shoes of the Chinese. Her father sat beside her in a three-piece suit with a high hat. In the dust and rumble of the rodeo, she became entranced by the progression of calves and steers, horses and bulls and men.

The roping and the bronc riding remained her favorite events. Agility, followed by power. She returned to the ranch house refreshed and in the coming weeks wrote poems of grit and enmity, provocation and release.

When she asked her father for a new horse, he shouted for joy. He'd brought her back to herself after all, making her walk with him if even in her own room. The horse would be her rebirth.

For a male colt he paid top dollar to the best quarter horse ranch in Montana.

A colt for her, gray-dappled with a black mane and forelegs. To Josef's delight she immediately took to the animal. She went to the colt daily, feeding him and rubbing him down. She smelled his face and combed him to get him used to people and touch. The horse was headstrong, a magnificent creature that would not be easy to break. She named him Imber. "Rain, in Latin," she explained, "sorrow." And certainly the horse would carry both her and her sorrow well, Josef thought.

IN THE EVENING Evelynne Lowry drew back the white lace curtains of her window upstairs to watch the horse feed in the fields. She'd met men of every shade of influence. Metal men, cattle kings, governors and railmen, senators, foresters, furriers, and bankers. These and their sons, the princes of men. Clearly her life had not followed a typical path, and in fact she'd never been smitten.

The next two men she encountered became indelible.

30.

WHEN HER HORSE matured, it was tall at the shoulder, broad in the chest and strong in the haunches, a darling to her but not yet broken and more than unwilling to be ridden. Josef hired a break man from the rodeo circuit, a bulldogger named Middie, a huge man known for his prowess with horses.

So big? Evelynne thought when she saw him, and she wondered at the hand of God. The man was a good bit taller than her father, who was already considered tall. He was twice as wide in the shoulders too, but not indelicate, she thought. He kept his head about him and held his hands with patience. His eyes revealed a sense of comfort with both mountains and plains. He was somewhat older than she, and she approved her father's selection.

She and the break man stood outside the corral in the lower field. Inside the ring Imber blew air from his nostrils, prancing, and shook his head. Twitchy, she thought. She wondered how the man would calm the horse. When her father came down from the house, the work would start.

"Missus," he said, looking at the horse. He touched the brim of his hat, wide-brimmed and clean, of white straw with a thin black band.

"Sir," she said, "you'll be breaking my horse. Don't break his will."

"Don't plan to," he said, removing his hat. His hair was light brown and close cut, his chin clean-shaven, his eyes blue.

The land was full of sounds, a chorus of birds, insects like cavalry in the grass, the wind through the trees. She studied the man.

He watched the ground at his feet.

"Fine horse, ma'am." Talking seemed awkward to him.

"Thank you," she said.

She folded her arms over the top rail and put the heel of her boot on the bottom rail. She wore a gray long skirt and black silver-buttoned vest over a white long-sleeved cotton blouse, pearl buttoned with a mandarin collar. No hat. Her hair was up. He looked at her neck more than her face. His clothes were rough, a rugged shirt more canvas than cotton, worn denim pants, and old boots. She noticed his fists, like large rocks slung at his sides.

Her father made his descent from the house, his boots like machinery stamping the earth. He wore spurs called the "Dandy" made by Guadalupe S. Garcia of Elko, Nevada. Heel chains, inlaid silver, curved shank, elaborate ornamentation, and sharp rowels.

"All right, now, go on," he called.

Middie moved slowly over the high rail, meeting the ground

on the other side with a grace that belied his size. He stood still, his head on a slant away from the horse. Saying little, they both watched him for a time, her arm hooked in her father's.

At last her father said, "Knows horses." He put his hand on her forearm. "Back to work now," he said, and kissed her cheek before he walked to the ranch house stiff-spined and intent.

"Name of this horse?" the man asked.

When she said, "Imber," the man cocked his ear.

"Imber," she said again.

"Learned from my Pappy's uncle," he said to the horse as much as her. Then he began to speak the name in soft tones. Gradually the horse grew less jumpy and stopped fidgeting. The horse was still now too, looking at the man. The man kept his back to the animal and walked away from the horse. The horse moved back and forth until the man paused, and the horse paused again. The man waited a long time before he kept walking again, and this time the horse followed at a distance.

Dust white over the corral, horse and man appeared to walk among clouds. Often the break man halted and just let the horse stand for what seemed to her a very long time. Past midday, the sun on an arc behind, she watched, saying nothing, as the horse seemed to be enjoying his circular walk with the man.

"Water?" she asked the break man.

"Thank you, missus," he said softly, the tone an octave or more below hers. She went thinking of this resonance and returned with a glass pitcher. He paused at the fence again, tipping his head back twice to drink as the horse stood behind him not an arm's length off.

The dance continued on and off throughout the day, with the

man taking long breaks to let the horse rest. The man waited an hour or more at a time now and didn't talk, but when he went back to work, he seemed glad. Evelynne found the movement compelling, something she'd happily see to its end. Watching him, she wanted to think of Tomás but would not let herself. Instead she listened to the cadence of the man's voice as he intoned "Imber" and the soft step of his boots in the dust.

The horse lifted a front hoof, pausing to eye the man, then lifted the hoof again before shaking his mane and moving where the man beckoned. By dark she made out the head and muzzle of her horse in the man's hands.

She pondered over how the break man worked without food and nearly without need and how the horse had simply come to him in the end while the man waited.

"That's it for today, ma'am."

"Can I give you some food for tonight?" she said.

"No, missus," he said. He put two fingers to his hat. "Thank you."

He walked from her down to the ranch house, where he untied and mounted his horse. Need to keep on, he thought. He disliked how hard it was for him to speak to a woman. The movement of men with women reminded him of cutting horses. No better way to see the power of a horse than in a neat and clean *stop*. The average cutting horse runs and runs, making all kinds of movement back and forth, but doesn't know when and where to stop. A great horse, though, like the blue roan he'd seen in a competition over near the Boulder River outside McLeod, makes a tremendous move and then stops. The horse knows the cow is held and simply holds the position, though the cow is in complete confusion, trying to return to the herd. No need to roar back and forth in a frenzy of muscle. Middie had seen it like a rare gem over in Sweet Grass County.

This woman could do that to him. Stop him cold.

"Tomorrow?" she called as he moved off into the dark among the trees.

"Tomorrow," he answered.

Evelynne shook her head. Amused, she walked around the fence in Imber's direction. She waited outside the corral and spoke to the animal. Her horse stood still and watched the forest.

BY WEEK'S END Imber took the bridle and bore the man's weight. By the time he was done it walked, trotted, cantered, galloped, and backed proficiently. "He'll need some getting used to you on him," he said when he handed her the reins, "you being so slight. But he'll go where you ask if you use your legs. Light on the rein. Firm nudge with the legs. He'll go anywhere you want to take him. Run him slow for a time. Gallop him when you're ready. No need for spurs or hard handling. Never much believed in it myself. Just lean or give him a press or a light heel."

She stared, her face stark. Words like a flood from him. She'd heard only "Imber" or short replies for fourteen days.

He looked at her now like she was fragile.

"I don't break," she said.

"Yes," he said.

"No," she said. "I mean I'm not delicate."

"No, ma'am," he said, lacing his hands together at his waist. "May I?"

She stepped into his open palms with her boot, took his shoulder, and swung into the saddle. When she hiked her skirt up to her thighs, Middie kept his eyes on her boot. She maneuvered her feet into the stirrups, taking the reins in her hands.

She couldn't help but think of Tomás. Her eyes teared. Her brother had never wished her to be unhappy. She had come up from exile to honor his life and to care for her father, though somehow it all seemed futile. Tomás had been the guardian of her hopes, but he'd died, she thought, trying to regain the tenderness he'd lost. She remembered how as a child Tomás had held her hand when they'd walked home from the upper field.

"Missus?" he said.

She rode at a canter to the upper field, where she and Tomás had played. Middie went to his own horse and followed her at a distance, watching her cross the rise up the hill into the tall grass where she flicked the reins and gave Imber his head. "Go," she said and tapped heels to the horse, and the horse leapt up before running wide open. She let him run hard all the way to the line of the forest perhaps a mile distant. There she slowed, turning gently until the animal leapt to again, flying over the field back in Middie's direction.

He marveled. Woman of bone and light, her hair let down over white, white skin. Her hair drawn by wind, the gray-black of the horse and the black-red of her hair above the shoulders of the horse like a fire. He admitted he had misjudged her. When she came close, he scanned only vaguely in her direction, though it was hard to keep his eyes off her.

"Fine work, missus," he said. He clenched the reins in a fist below the bit and held Imber's muzzle, sensing in the horse's eyes a kind of pride.

"Fine piece of riding," he said.

She looked down at him with his hand on the horse.

"Evelynne," she said and put her hand out. "Evelynne Lowry."

"Zion," he said, enclosing her hand in his.

"The horse responds." She patted the horse's neck with her other hand. "Thank you."

"He does," Zion answered, releasing her.

"Fine day," he said finally, but he felt the fool, like he'd crossed an unforeseen line.

"Yes," she said. His hold here will be slight now, she thought.

"Best be going," he said.

"I should have need for you to stay on a while to be sure of the break," she said.

He looked at her then, directly.

"A man can't abide unnecessary work," he said.

"The work is surely necessary," she answered. "It will make my father happy to know I'm safe. Besides, I can learn from your way with horses."

"You're safe as they come, missus. With that horse and how you ride."

"I ask you kindly, Zion," she said and did not turn away. "My father's mind will be soothed if you stay."

He waited.

"Have your man send for me in town if it's your father's wish," he said finally.

He mounted his horse.

"Yes." She touched her horse's forelock and nodded to him.

Zion tipped his hat. "Missus," he said. He looked at her horse. "Imber." The horse's ears rotated slightly before it lowered its head to pull grass.

Strange name for a horse, he thought as he rode away. But pretty enough, and suits the animal. A name a woman might give.

Evelynne Lowry.

He'd heard of her in Butte. Tales over cards and whiskey. The men knew largely nothing of her but said she was a hermit who didn't think straight. Crazed, they said, and mean. He found her nothing like the ill vision they gave. He was glad he'd paid for a bath, haircut, and shave.

For her part, Evelynne felt something for him. She saw kindness in him like her brother. She'd keep her thoughts close, not to be given to him or anyone. She needed to be sure her father didn't read them in her either.

Zion. The man's name was Zion.

City on a hill. A citadel, she thought. A good name. A very strong name.

31.

MIDDIE RODE INTO town and down Main Street before he went north into the mountains, where he made camp. Below him the great city of Butte glimmered, a full-fledged town graced with theaters and luxury hotels, fine restaurants, horse racing, gambling, and a high-end amusement park. Across the hill wooden and steel head frames served as doors to mines that dug deep caverns in the earth.

The town boasted hundreds of saloons. Along Wyoming Street houses of prostitution thrived, the lavish Dumas Brothel and Venus Alley, where women plied their trade in thin-framed cribs, a line of double-decked openings attached to the back walls of buildings, fronted by a curtain, a single lightbulb over each entrance. He'd heard of underground tunnels where the bulk of the whoring went on in caves.

After dark he sat on his haunches on the mountainside that looked over the city. He took his mother's ivory comb from the chest pocket of his shirt, holding it in his hands. He knew to keep his own solitude. He stared at the horizon, where a gap through the narrows carved a trough in the sky. Her father had money and power. Middie would be at his ease when he was away from the man. He felt a duty to the horse, though, and, if he would allow himself, to the woman.

At length he kicked dirt over the fire and watched the smoke drift until the gray column of it thinned and there was nothing but black. He laid out his bedroll, feeling his body sink until he slept. He dreamed of horse's hooves in flight, a locomotive pulling a line of coal smoke in knuckled billows from its top hat. A horse moved hard alongside the cars, and he saw a woman's face pressed to a glass window before the animal outdistanced the passenger cars, then the engine, and Middie rode alone across an empty plain where rail ties set a line to the end of seeing.

He woke in a sweat before sitting upright on his haunches again as he held his knees in his arms and looked out at the night. He'd stay on two days, no more, he told himself.

IN THE DARK she sat at her vanity in her bedroom above the staircase to the great room. The exhilaration was still high in her chest, Imber being more than she expected and the giant still more. Again she wondered at the work of God. The unutterable shades and lights of creation. Lions and wolverines, bobcat and lynx. Nighthawks, eagles, and red-winged blackbirds. White birch, devil's club, buckwheat, glacier lily. Timothy coated in a glove of hoarfrost.

She hadn't really looked on a man since before her brother's death, since before even the hard treatment Tomás had endured from their father over the woman in St. Louis. She remembered she and Tomás used to race at length through fields thick with wildflowers, the horses chest high in camas and fireweed. A heady scent rode high in the honeysuckle as they sped down coulees and up the steppe to the higher plateau, where the mountainside was lush and plumes of beargrass on yellow stalks looked like torches. She had forgotten what it meant to give a horse its legs. No more, she told herself. She went from her room to the mirror in the hall to look at herself full length. Her father approached from the stairs. He put his hands on her shoulders as he viewed her image, distinct and of unsettling beauty.

"So like your mother. So very spirited," he said. "Just like her."

"I rode today," she said.

He turned from her, descending the stairs. "Chan Wu told me," he called over his shoulder before he went to the writing table, where he picked up his fountain pen among scattered papers. "Makes a father glad." He sat down to continue his work. "Very glad indeed." He raised his head. "Chan was ecstatic," he said. "But stay away from that hand. I see your eyes for him."

"Yes, father," she called from the railing before turning to the mirror again, wistful as she beheld the blush in her face. Her brother was right. Her father would brook no resistance. Nor would he consider her feelings. She pursed her lips. The break man outsized him. Zion, a man rare in expanse and unafraid of other men but who in fact seemed to fear women. He spoke straight. He didn't let on what happened behind his eyes. She liked him very much.

32.

THE NEXT DAY, when Zion took her through his paces with the horse, she saw his apprehension. She thanked him at day's end, and after he'd gone she waited until long after dark. Near upon midnight, with her father passed out from Kentucky bourbon, she stole from the house. Chan had told her about the man's fighting, and she wanted to see for herself. Chan accompanied her as she walked in dark clothing, her face veiled, in the alley behind the Hungry Horse Saloon off Main Street. She placed her hand in his arm, feeling secure with him as he led her up a dirt incline to a peek hole in the slats, a gap about the width of a horseshoe and head high that gave a view of a dirt floor below, a room walled with men.

Bare-chested, the break man moved in the middle with a calmness to him but also a pain in his eyes that made her press her face to the opening. Zion sent one man after the next to the ground. A single strike to the face with his fist, a forearm to the chest, or, hands clasped, a double-armed blow to the back. She was surprised any of them rose the way they collapsed at his feet. But water was thrown in their faces, and they staggered up as their friends hauled them away, groggy-eyed, steeped in misdirection. She told Chan to go home, but he refused. When she grew hostile, he finally walked away from her, but only to a position at the near corner of the building. With her hand on the wood slats she glanced at Chan again, a flurry of moths above him at the light that horned out from the wall where he stood. Finally she saw the giant accept a small roll of bills before he walked out the front doors.

From a distance she followed on horseback, quiet among the side streets with Chan unseen in the shadows. She heard fiddle music in the dark, lonesome and abiding. Her horse carried her to where Zion made his way out of town, and she kept on until she saw him halt and make camp partway up the mountain. She quieted her horse, Chan behind her as if invisible.

She led Imber into the small circle where he kept his fire. He didn't start.

"Fancy you're here," Zion said.

"Saw you fight in town," she said.

"Not fit for a woman." He sat on the ground, wrapping his knees in his arms. Opening his hands, he pressed them down over the tops of his boots. The ball his body made was outsized, his form more boulder than man.

"Fit for me," she said. Watching him, she felt some fear.

"You reckon?" he said. He didn't like the hardness in his voice. He felt awkward in her presence here on the end of night. She was kind enough, if forward, but her father would not approve.

His men would come, and the mess Middie made of them would ruin his welcome. He generally avoided women. He'd spoken to a few, one in Bozeman, another in Missoula, a Sioux girl in Wolf Point. He even thought perhaps he might like to have married the Sioux girl, but he never could put enough words together to make his feelings known, and he came back always to the realization of the fear they brought him and how he wasn't sure he'd be different than his own father.

Yet here he was with Evelynne Lowry.

Certainly she was a nearly perfect work of creation, he thought. He felt near to his mother when she spoke. He thought her well designed, like a lavender cone of lupine. He kept still, letting her aspect wash over him.

She saw his body resolve then, the broad lay of his shoulders and his back as his posture softened. His face was not badly wounded, a simple unpronounced mark of red over his right cheekbone and two nicks above the right eye. "I've traveled back east," she said. Her voice wavered slightly as he watched her. What was she doing here? She looked over her shoulder and did not see Chan but hoped he was not far off. The bed of Zion's eyes was dark. "New York, Washington, D.C., Boston. Cities that house so many people you can't count them and you can't get away from them. They press into each other like grains of sand in a wash."

"I expect so," he said, his arms still wrapped around his knees.

She touched his shoulder.

"Will you stand?" she said.

"Yes, missus," he answered, and standing, he towered over her. In the dim light his eyes looked burdened. He hopes for more than his own life, she thought. He placed his hand on the out-side of her arm. "Best be going," he said. Light scent in the air of grass and trees. The touch propelled her toward him, and he leaned down.

When she drew his face to her and kissed his mouth, he pulled away.

"Zion," she said.

She was vexed and thought she might cry and shout all at once. She tried to steady herself, but fright had taken him. He moved quickly now, untying the reins of his horse as he looked back at her, his eyes white. When he heeled the horse, it jumped forward, fleeing through the trees in a ruckus.

What had she done? She put her face in her hands. In the dis-tance she heard the hooves of his horse and snapped deadfall. She shivered. Far off a path of dust billowed behind him as the horse met a game trail and descended the mountain like some-thing shot from the barrel of a gun. He had left his camp and bedroll.

Staring at the distance, she questioned herself. She felt ashamed. She'd envisioned herself convincing Zion and him stealing her away from her father. Zion was freedom. She was not ready. Not at all prepared. She needed to get home. Chan would be in the woods behind her.

She was sad for her father and for herself. The days ahead will lead away from this town, she thought. The rims of her eyes stung. She knew she needed to go, but under circumstances more secure than this.

She took a path among the trees above Butte, back toward home. Near the descent that led to the upper meadow, Chan's horse joined hers. Chan said nothing as the horses walked to-gether. Near the barn he drew his horse close to hers. "This your father cannot discover. I fear for you." His eyes were pained. She bowed her head and he bowed his, a shared disgrace under which she thanked him for accompanying her. As she went to the house Chan watched her before taking her horse to the stable.

When she passed behind the house she took off her boots on the veranda before entering through the back door in her stock-ing feet. She walked into the kitchen, where she heard her fa-ther's low snore through the walls. She sighed as she took the staircase to the upper hall and to her bedroom. She undressed then put on her nightclothes and emerged again, walking the long hall to her father's room. From the open doorway she saw the rise and fall of his breathing. He lay on his back under a thick covering, his form ensconced in moonlight. His gray-black pom-padour rose above the roman outline of his face.

She touched his forehead. His breathing was heavy-laden. She kept her hand on his head for a long time before she returned to her bedroom, went to the window and watched the night.

She wondered if Zion had come back to his place on the mountain. His flight has harmed me, she thought. Tears met her cheeks. I am unworthy of love, she told herself, recognizing the thought as one she'd had since birth. She felt torn in two. She didn't need Zion. She also didn't want the life of a spinster. She was willing to die, she thought, even for someone she didn't know. But if a man might love her, which she considered both delightful and perilous, she questioned how in God's heaven she might love that man in return without fitting him for the whip of her family, her father.

For some days she thought of Zion, but as time passed she heard nothing. In the end she put the moment away, sealing it like a relic encased in glass. She wanted a man who would be a true gift, as she would be to him, a strength to buffer the tyranny of her father. She saw the bulwark of Zion's body, the quiet in his eyes. She had wanted very much to love him, she thought. But he was gone. So she would release him.

Day followed night and night day: a month, a handful of months, a year, but as thoughts of Zion lingered, she was surprised at the force they held. In the end she simply pushed the memories more forcefully off. Beholding her face in the mirror, she found herself ugly or untoward. What hope she had of escaping her father faded before it finally blinked out.

BLACK KETTLE

33.

WILLIAM BLACK KETTLE stepped on a robin's egg, and what lay beneath his boot now was something he didn't want to see. Loosely bundled sticks at the base of a fence post, no real nest, nothing for safety or provision. He'd been looking over the rodeo grounds when he heard the crunch and felt the egg flatten under the ball of his foot. He folded his arms on the fence rail, resting his head as he watched the white riders with their toothy grins. More often than not, he thought, wherever they went they took what they wanted. Most despised him or anyone not white.

He didn't like to hate, but he hated their claim on this land.

Regardless, what he saw humbled him. He and the white men, and Raymond with them, ran horses while they roped. They put up corrals together. They organized rodeo grounds, feeding their animals from the same thatch of hay. Indian men and white men at play whose father's fathers had been at war. As Raymond pushed cattle into the chutes with two white men, William questioned if men could find their way.

Over a gap along the far side of the stock corral, he saw her.

He hooded his eyes to take in the view: a range of mountains, rock faces skirted by forests, and through the oblique angle of the shadow his hand made, a woman who walked like she owned the world.

The wine-colored dress met the woman's body and gave a crispness to her torso. Her neck was white. She wore a maroon wide-brimmed hat veiled in white muslin. Behind her ear he made out the black-red sheen of her hair. Her face was pretty, serious, and somber. He wanted to speak with her directly, but the white man's Montana was no place for an Indian to talk to a white woman.

She walked toward a large grandstand. The rodeo grounds were nicely fenced with an out-chute at the back of the field along with livestock chutes up at the start point. In small towns you made do, no fence to shield the goings-on, a ring of carriages and an automobile or two. Often people just had to get out of the way when the broncs or bulls went wild. Here the town prided itself on a good rodeo. The grandstand was even covered by a large rectangular roof.

On her way she paused and carefully eyed the horses tied to the upper rail. She approached them each in their turn. The Chinese men who were her attendants stood a stone's throw off, waiting.

William felt the braid at the base of his neck and touched the thick bole of it from habit, making sure it ran down his back beneath his shirt. He gripped the crown of his cowboy hat. Firming the hat to his head, he set off toward her. Behind the chutes he heard the cows in their monotonous mutter and groan. He spoke to them as he walked, "Yes, boss. Good bossy, bossy," moving as if aimless toward the cluster of horses where the top of her hat stood out among them. "Cheyenne," a man called from behind, but William kept on until he found himself walking on the far side of the stock chutes among a few buckskins, paints, and bays, a sorrel and an appaloosa. When he ducked under the neck of a big white horse with black spots, he came into her presence, and she whispered, "Halt, please," stopping him abruptly. "I'm sorry," she said as she turned to him. "I mean, how do you do?" She reached out her hand.

Staring at her, he felt unable to move.

"We shake," she said, and he slowly took her hand and shook it.

"Yes," he said, feeling his blood return. He smiled, striding past her, but then turned back and stood before her again.

We come into new ground, she thought. Her lips went cold. She'd never been a hater of Indians. In fact she found the Indian's presence here a lovely disturbance. She glanced over her shoulder, where she met Chan's eyes among the other Chinese men. He smiled. She turned back to the Indian. William stepped closer, saying, "You're very natural with them," as he placed a hand on the shoulder of the large spotted horse beside her. He watched her face intently. "You love their strength," he said.

"I do," she said, "though they get temperamental."

"They do," he agreed. The stilted quality between them diminished. She took another step forward. She looked over her shoulder again. She would court disaster. They looked on one another for a moment until she averted her gaze.

Tipping her hat, she hid her eyes and said, "Good day."

"Good day," he responded, and she went her way then, walking with her attendants to the grandstand, where she seated herself to watch the festivities.

He knew what he was about to do. He touched his hand to his hair, then followed her, mounting the narrow walk-up to the grandstand, striding lightly, almost wind-like, in her direction. Finally he ascended three wide steps. She saw him coming and didn't know what to think but admired his tall frame and confident gait, especially here where people would have their minds churning up silt about him as if from a dark river.

34.

"Good day to you again, madam," he said.

She did not turn to him this time.

The Chinese, all twelve in black, looked straight ahead. Chan sat two men to the left of her. Black Kettle stepped forward and sat down beside her. Dust rose from the rodeo ground. The men of the arena looked in his direction and grimaced as if their faces had been punched with iron. It would be now or not at all, he thought. Smiling again, she looked at him before touching her hand to her hat. The arena paused as they reckoned him and her. He'd put up a fight with these men, she thought. She put out her hand. They shook politely in front of everyone, and the simple gesture settled it as the cowboys went back to rodeo doings, only eyeing them on occasion, perhaps to make sure what they saw was real.

Removing his hat, William placed it on the bench beside him.

"Thank you," he said.

"My pleasure." She motioned to the men of the arena. "They're watchful because of my father."

"Your father?"

The sun was behind her. His face caught the light. She saw he parted his hair down the middle and pulled it back to the braid that went beneath his collar. Not many Indians in this area of the state, she thought. She faintly recalled an Indian hand on the ranch when she was a child. She'd been to powwows with her father and was more curious and concerned for the Indian than herself. She liked the textured look of his hair. Her father was in D.C., or the present meeting would not be taking place.

"He's protective," she said.

"You're a grown woman," William said, smiling. The English in his mouth felt smooth and made him happy to speak with her. A rare gladness, talking with a white woman.

"You're also very beautiful," he continued.

"Thank you," she said, laughing lightly as she tipped her hat again. Her father would in no way abide this, a man speaking openly with her, let alone an Indian. At the powwows her father had walked with her in a quarry of white men, and the vitriol had dripped from their lips. To her father and his own, Indians were less than men. But this man smelled good to her, like sage.

She thought of Chan. He was a safe haven, a fortress. A listener, a quiet speaker. She watched him now. He stared straight forward, his body at ease. Always he wanted the best for her. She reached and touched the Indian's hair for a moment before she drew her hand away. The hair was coarse. She felt she'd transgressed him. As a child, when she'd touched Chan's hair, his had been smooth. "I don't mean to offend," she said. "Your hair is very long."

"No offense taken," William said.

He smiled. His teeth looked white as milk. She found his eyes pleasant. She hated to think of her father's response had he seen her touch the Indian's hair. He would want to bruise her. He would desire the man dead.

She eyed the braid at the back of the Indian's neck.

"Is it to your waist?" she asked.

"Yes," he said. "From when I was a boy." He touched her forearm before placing his hand back in his lap. "The hair is long unless we are in mourning," he said. She thought of Tomás, of her own hair done up inside her hat and how she too had wanted it shorn when he'd died, but she'd merely stayed far from people and had no will.

"I see," she said.

She looked out at the arena, at the men on the outside against the far fence. She paid them no mind.

William lifted his braid out of his shirt collar and held it to her.

"May I?" she said.

"Of course," he said, the sound of his laughter like silver coins dropped on a table.

A black rope, she thought, tied at the end by a simple blue cloth. She knew she should try to protect this man from herself, and from her father, but she was intrigued.

"May I?" he said, and she startled as he nodded to her hat, her hair. She handed the braid back, and he tucked it in his shirt again.

"May I?" he asked again.

She faced him now, steeled her eyes, and said, "Yes."

Taking her hat off, she placed it beside her, pulled a series of pins, and undid her hair so that it flowed to its length along her back and down beside her face to her lap.

He opened his hand and let it run down the back of her hair.

"Nice," he said.

She found his smile beautiful.

In the faces of the men below, she saw disgust. In fact their eyes brewed rage. He was not oblivious. He spoke to her anyway. "Akin to my own," he said. "Nearly the same, but thicker. Not so full of sunlight as mine, though." He winked at her. She couldn't help it. She laughed out loud.

He was a man who spoke to a woman, delighting her with his words. He had touched her hair openly. He was not afraid. But she questioned her own resolve. For all her pluck, still she was undone by the distance between women and men. Her jaw tightened. How could she be so strong and so fearful at once? Everyone in town would know she had sat with the Indian today, even if he was nothing to her. She thought of her brother. The touch of a woman, rare and deadly. She placed her hands in the folds of her dress.

"Your name?" she asked.

"Black Kettle," he replied.

"A strange name," she said, "and lovely."

"My great-great-grandfather's name," he said. "A peace chief."

"Peace?" she said.

"Among the tribes," he said. "Between the whites and the Cheyenne."

She looked at him now. "Lovelier still."

"My Christian name is William," he said. "Given by my mother in honor of a half-white, half-Cheyenne man who lived with the tribe."

She smiled more with William than she'd smiled in years. His speech was fluid, his eyes were charming. Despite herself, she touched his arm. She hadn't laughed for so long.

With the men below her alerted, she knew she needed to move now before the encounter went to where it might beckon violence. "You must go," she said, and she smiled on him with kindness. "Or I must go." She nodded at the men. "They will not be happy. They'll speak to my father."

He saw the cowboys' faces, most of them turned in his direction. He knew they wouldn't let him leave this place without trying to exact a punishment. He looked back at her. He did not let his eyes move from hers.

"Until we meet again," he said, placing his hand on his hat. Then he walked back down to the grounds, around the horses toward the chutes. As he went she lifted her hat to shade her eyes. His movements were uncommon, and elegant. Like an eagle, she thought, or a lion on the mountain. He was long, and he moved with ease. His face had been a wonder of invitation.

She pinned her hair, tucked it into her hat again, and watched the rodeo.

35.

WHEN WILLIAM ROUNDED the cattle chutes, he found Raymond leaned up against a fence post. He chewed snoose, watching William like he was a crazy dog. As William drew closer, Killsnight's teeth greeted him with a grin and a sound like the nicker of a horse.

"Close your lips," William said.

"What?" Raymond said, still grinning.

"What's so funny?" William said. "Haven't you ever seen a woman?"

"A woman," said Raymond, "yes. But a white woman sitting with a Cheyenne boy at a rodeo, never. That, my pink Indian friend, is something to get us killed."

Killsnight viewed William cockeyed until William finally gave him his eyes. "Too bold," Raymond said, "going up there with her in front of everyone. Especially here. Especially that woman." He pointed his nose in her direction. "We will need to cut town directly after we rope," Raymond said. "No man here will let us go without a fight. If we rope and ride out, we leave with our skins." He peered at William as if begging him to comply.

William stared hard at Raymond's face. "Yes," he said finally, "we'll do as you say."

Raymond punched William in the chest, and they both looked up, staring at her again. "Take some chaw," Raymond said as he opened a small leather pouch of shredded tobacco, giving some to William before he put another plug in his own cheek.

Then they went out and won so handsomely that the competition looked more like children than men. Upon leaving the arena, William thought he saw her wave from her phalanx of Chinese.

"Tonight, Cheyenne," a grizzled old-timer said as they dismounted. He spit on the ground at their feet, and William said, "Yes," as they walked the horses past the man and around the corner of the bandstand. At the stock chutes, another man said, "Watch yourself," as he sat on the top rail over the steers. Others looked in their direction as William and Raymond walked the horses through town as if nothing were afoot. They went steadily east until the landscape swallowed them and none could discern where they'd gone.

Her final words to him in the grandstand stayed with him: You must go, or I must go. The directness of her voice. Hope in the blood, he thought, as if she meant to say, "You may never see me again, my father forbids you," and at the same time "Come to me and make me your own."

36.

WILLIAM AND RAYMOND went east to Columbus, Absorokee, and finally Billings. They won at every stop, wowed crowds, and heard the people calling out.

"Hot damn," the men said. "Lightning!"

Onlookers tipped their hats.

"Quick and clean," said one old-timer, "like the strike of a rattler."

As they worked a steer in tight tandem, the harmony of horse and rope brought a tide of admiration. In daylight they received accolades, and money when they won.

After dark it wasn't the same. Men sought them in the saloons or the streets to lord it over them, to take their earnings or try to beat them down in cards or fisticuffs. Generally the two avoided contact with white men.

On the rare occasion when they were cornered, they feint-ed and found their way into the darkness or stayed, holding their own, William a man of slender face and high-boned torso, wide shoulders over a thin waist and long-muscled frame, and Raymond blocky with a squarish jaw and body mass more broad-chested than barrel. They grew increasingly more skilled at the foresight required to avoid people and places that reeked of foul reckoning.

37.

ON A RISE above the Yellowstone River outside Billings, they laid their bedrolls on dry grass beneath the shade of a large splayed cottonwood among a few others that grew up from the river. In early release the trees hung small tails of cotton in the leaves, and the seed floated on the air like a slow flurry of snow along the river. William and Raymond unsaddled, watering the horses before letting them loose to graze. They filled their water pouches and took a long draft, then lay down in the shade, their hats over their faces as they slept.

The hats were well used, of brown wool felt that kept the skull warm.

William's hat still had a little stiffness to the brim.

Raymond's was beaten all to hell.

The sun bled the afternoon through as they lay with their arms crossed at the chest, their legs straight out like dead men. Near dusk they rose under the westward burn of a cloudless sky and gathered a store of old sagebrush roots and pies of cow dung, setting a flame that fired quickly with a rich scent.

They had done well, winning in Billings to the delight of a crowd of whites, quite a few Crow, and some Cheyenne.

"Home," William said as he fed the fire and gazed at the river, a blue-brown, big-bodied flow that churned among rim rocks, winding itself east. Cotton drifted overhead. "Good life, rodeo-ing," he said. Raymond sat on a tree root, looking out. William wondered if Raymond thought of his father, Bull. "Always pretty much good eating," William continued, "and a little money to bring home and help."

Raymond nodded, smiling. "Hard riding," he said. "More than our fair share of wins."

William remembered a time when their winning had been threatened, when his horse had gone ill of a long wound to the flank from a fence at the Assiniboine and Sioux rodeo in Poplar. At home he'd taken the horse to the old man who had a sack of medicine for horse-curing. The animal's head was low. Film covered its eyes. In the gray light the old man faced the horse east and put some of the medicine, made of small leafy plants, into his own mouth before he came close and spit into the palm of his right hand. He touched the an-imal's nose with the paste, rubbing it around the nostrils as he shook and pulled the right ear, then the left. The old man walked around to the right side, spitting more medicine into his hand, then rubbing it on the shoulder and the hip, over the bloody wound on the flank, then to the shoulder and hip on the other side the same way before going clear around again to the tail. He pulled the tail four times as the horse lifted its head and snorted. The animal took its time but healed even stronger than before.

William gathered a large flat rock from the river, let it dry, and placed it over the outer coals. When the heat came up in the stone, he opened his satchel and prepared bannock bread with a fist of flour, some shortening with salt, and a spot of sugar. He pulled a slab of jerked pronghorn from the satchel. Tearing it in two, he gave half to Raymond. Raymond acknowledged him with a tip of his nose.

As night fell a harvest moon came up in the west, and when the coyotes began their singsong, the two friends sat on their heels and sang too. Flats spread from the other side of the river south. Foxes roamed the sage, their eyes lit disks on occasion at the edge of the firelight. Finally they lay back with their heads on their bedrolls.

"I'm sorry about your father," said William.

Raymond nodded. "My heart hurts for my mother and me," he said. "We miss him."

Raymond turned to William.

"He did you wrong," Raymond said, "though once he loved you as he loved me."

"I wish he was still here," said William.

"Me too," said Raymond.

"You are welcome in my family," William said, "always."

Looking at the fire, Raymond nodded. "And you in mine."

The saddles lay on the ground near the bedrolls, their guns in leather-fringed casings over the saddles. The bows that were constant for them as boys were long unused now, bundled and stored by their mothers with the women's old buffalo robes and bone needles and the boys' cradleboards.

The guns were octagon-barrel Winchesters purchased with some months' wages as hands for the white ranches north of the reservation. Their fathers' old Remingtons remained home in the lodges. The Winchesters they had bought used at a gun show in Rock Springs outside Miles City. William eyed the rifles, the barrels covered but angled upward. He was proud of those guns. Twelve dollars well spent to keep them and their families fed. Ammunition at one dollar a box. He and Raymond cared for those weapons as they would a child.

In the white lands they faced curses along with blows of boot and fist. They were revered by the People, William thought, for what they earned, respect and dignity, money, medals, belts, buckles—and they were given gifts in return. His mother's gifts were the sweetest, beaded moccasins and fringed leggings, gloves with beaded gauntlets, the soft scabbards that held the Winchesters. With the whites he had one change of clothes. With his mother he had abundance.

They let the fire go down. William loved day's end, the turn of night and the way their voices went low and how the memories of home called to them. He remembered his father catching eagles at the heights of the mountains, his stories of how he lay silent in the pit, the meat of deer or rabbit placed on full-growth branches overhead. When the eagle came down, William's father leapt up and gripped the bird's ankle, feeling the knife of the talons. He said the fight was unlike any a man would have in this life. The eye of the bird, hot and fearless, was never forgotten.

38.

IN THE MORNING they rode along the foothills of the Big Horn Mountains of Wyoming on the southern line of the Crow lands. Far below, the blue coil of the river was encased in high-walled rock. The Cheyenne territory lay farther east. They shot two pronghorn to bring to the tribe, leaving the horses off distant before kneeling to touch the heads of the antelope and speak gratitude. In less than an hour they boned out the animals, taking the backstraps and rib meat, wrapping the quarters along with the other edibles in the antelope hides. The inedibles, the hooves and skull, body cage, and spine, they left for crow and coyote, insect and magpie. Blood covered their forearms. They left it alone, licking at their hands as they rode. The remains would be a white ribwork behind them until the bones bleached, falling again to grass and soil.

They came bearing wool coats and pants for the old ones, coffee and coffee pots tied above the bedrolls. They passed the place where the Cheyenne and Sioux killed Custer. Yellow Hair with a head of fool's gold. They entered camp at night to the glow of the tipi fires, and soon a high skunk fire was set in the center circle, where William and Raymond were welcomed heartily. William's mother and father along with Raymond's mother drew near, embracing them, touching the young men's faces and hair. Then they all feasted together with much dancing and song.

The next day in the afternoon the two bathed in the Tongue with William's father, Georgie, before William and Raymond placed their white man's clothes in the trees to dry and to be put away in the lodge along with their hard-soled boots. Shirts, leggings, and moccasins from their mothers were brought out for them.

William's mother braided his hair, tying the ends with colored cloth. When he slept in the lodge again that night, she held the curve of his head. Praying over him, she called him her son. She also touched the back of Georgie's head and called him father of her son, singing her songs into the deep dark.

ZION

39.

AFTER EVELYNNE'S KISS Zion backtracked to retrieve his belongings before riding hard north. He spent time avoiding the thoughts that formed like a web in his mind. He fought and drifted, worked day labor, and rodeoed intermittently, making a circuitous route. He was never at rest, never long in one place, but finally, after much hard bulldogging and hand work, he arrived back near Heart Butte, where he sought out the old Blackfeet woman. He had thought of returning east on the Highline to the town where his mother had died, but couldn't seem to get himself to go back. Instead he came through the open expanse west before Heart Butte, bringing the old woman a bag of flour, a fancy hat with lace trim, two beaver pelts, and a muskrat.

He stayed a month with her. He reckoned he would stay on until he could think again, but the worry rode his mind without relief. So he went south toward Missoula under double rainbows that arched over half the sky. He would cut above the Clark Fork and Bitterroot Rivers and the Hell's Gate Canyon, he told himself. He'd make his way back to where Evelynne had claimed him.

He was still some days' ride outside Butte, camped on the edge of a forest where the land fell away and the valley opened on night, when her voice seemed to come to him in a whisper. She was a visage from which he could not escape, her face, her eyes so sharply green that to gaze on them was to be laid down in tall grass. He wished she had been able to meet his mother. As he tended the fire his eyes watered. Who breathes the stars into place, he thought, and gives a woman to be so fearfully and wonderfully made? The horse's muzzle nudged his back. Zion rose, taking the horse to graze before he spread his bedroll and slept.

A FEW HOURS' ride from Butte he stopped in a field of blue camas that reached ahead of him in a wind that made the earth appear to shift and move. The flowers went all the way to a line of pine that led down a swale into a broad, wedge-shaped river valley. On the path behind him he'd joined the Silver Bow west of the confluence of Bearmouth and Blacktail Creeks. There he'd paused to watch a cow moose and her calf on the edge of the river. They chewed horsetail and pondweed as a bull with enormous spoon antlers swam head-high through the water to the other side. Zion moved below the tree line, following the river east and south among lodgepole and dwarf fir until he came out at last into this broad field robed in basin flowers of a beauty near painful to the eye.

A day back, in Boulder, he'd bought a change of clothes and

burned his old ones. He bathed in a small glacial lake and rubbed his skin raw with the block soap he'd purchased at the Boulder general store. A haircut, beard removal, and the new clothes took nearly all his money.

Now he walked his horse through the blue field until he reached the river's edge. The pressure in him made him want to turn back, but he thought of his mother and wouldn't allow himself. She'd smile to see him here, touch his face, move him on the way.

He tried to ignore the booming in his chest.

40.

WHEN HE DROPPED through a gap in the trees above the ranch house his body shook and he breathed out to let it pass. He moved his horse into the high grass that led to her father's holdings. He let the horse eat. Down the draw stood the house, a structure set out like an arm, vaulted on the central ridgeline. The wraparound porch framed the first floor as if anchoring it to the height above. Beyond the house were the stables in the lower field, and below all an oxbow valley spread wide where the river curved among mountains. He took the reins again and trotted through the meadow. He steadied the horse firmly so the animal wouldn't get jaunty and the horse moved smooth as water into the low grass where the house lay. He came around the north-west corner to the midpoint where the front doors stood open.

When he dismounted, he tied reins to rail and walked to the landing where he strode through the opening onto a span of wood floor and framed ceiling that reached overhead four times the length of a man. The banister of the second floor was set at the back. The skull mounts of moose, deer, and antelope adorned the room as well as three mountain goats and an elk, whose rack he stood directly to the right of, which reached from above his head nearly to the rafters. On a table to his right a bear skull was framed on velvet in a circle of claws. Faint odors filled the room, of glue and tack, hair and bone.

No one greeted him.

He stood for a time before he called out, "Mr. Lowry, sir?"

He heard a rustling upstairs, then a woman's voice.

"He's gone to Butte today." She emerged at the railing. "You looking for work?" she said, but when she recognized him, her face went grave. She came round and stood at the height of the stairs.

Her neck and face were flushed.

The fright rose in him, of an engagement in such close quarters. Her presence alone could overcome his will.

"Ma'am," he said to the ground. He heard the rustle of her dress as she descended the stair until she stood a length away from him. He took his hat off, worrying it with his hands.

Grace, he thought, like water from the mountain. He held his ground but did not look up at her face and fine nose, her black hair with a hint of red.

"I'm here," he said, staring at his feet as if to keep them in place.

"I'm glad," she said quietly. She beheld him, telling herself she would need to be much more careful so as not to be disgraced again.

"Yes, missus," he said, as the heat rose in his neck.

He is here, she thought. Here again, before me. She felt lost. Her hands were chill as snow. No one could aid her now, she thought, she must provide her own assistance.

"Go," she said.

He raised his head.

"Meet me in the draw above the ridge." She pointed with her face to the mountain above the field. "I will follow."

He stared at her blankly.

She clenched the cloth on the sides of her dress. Zion left without another word.

From the upper window she watched the horse skirt the field at a canter, enter the forest, and move steadily upward through the trees.

She retrieved her riding boots from the hall. When she called to Chan, he emerged from the kitchen, bowed, and smiled kindly before he went to prepare her horse.

IN THE DRAW Zion stood beside his horse. She descended the terrain, dismounted, and let Imber graze. Zion kept his distance. She kept hers. The mountain was behind them. They said nothing. Her head felt pressed down, her frame fragile. She could outwill her father by coming here against him, but it seemed now with Zion so near she had no will. She questioned her own indiscretion.

"Will you speak?" she said. The effort halted her breathing.

"Yes'm," he said, followed by silence.

She shook her head and exhaled.

But he didn't speak. The man was a steel trap, she thought. She took a step toward him. He shied from her.

Zion set his heels into the ground. Stay put, he told himself. The sweat on his hands felt like rain. He pushed his palms against the front of his denims. She needed words, but he had no words. If she took another step, he'd bolt.

She didn't take another step. Tucking his chin to his chest, he stared out at her from below the bones of his eyes. Her gaze took him in. She had a very puzzled look.

"Say something," she insisted.

She was between him and his horse.

"What is it?" she asked, her voice quavering.

She waited to see what might come, but when still he said nothing, she turned toward her horse and mounted, positioning herself in the saddle before she faced him again.

"It is best we meet in town tonight after my father sleeps," she said. She hoped a little time might create some comfort. "Behind the Hungry Horse Saloon," she said, "past midnight."

The same place she'd seen him fight before.

She rode past him. He wanted to reach and touch her arm. She halted her horse a pace beyond. "Will you meet me?"

"Yes," he said.

She rode out of the draw, down the mountain.

He stood where he was, cursing himself. He couldn't see being able to give her, or any woman, what she deserved.

He worked to calm himself as the horse grazed. On the ground near his feet, he saw the small cup of a flowering bitterroot, pink with a near red heart, flared as if having pushed through rock. He walked to his horse and rode east.

ON THE FINAL descent toward Butte the industry of the city presented itself like the jointed legwork of an infestation: carriages and cars, mine heads and not a few cranes, people moving hither and yon at a quick pace.

As he entered the outskirts men stared. When he saw their alarm, he remembered his size and cursed himself again. As he passed into an alley he parted a handful of Indians, a mix of Blackfeet and Cree, he thought. They stared at the shoulders and flanks of his horse. As he rode on they smiled, clicking their tongues.

When he took a chair in a corner of the Hungry Horse, the tender came to him squint-eyed, sliding a whiskey slug into his hand across a small circular table. "Paying customers," he said. Zion eyed the tender, a potbellied stove of a man with a long neck and sparse hair, someone unknown to him. The grind in the man's face flattened under Zion's gaze. "You're good for it," the tender said and went away.

I'll fight tonight, Zion thought. Pay the man then. He was merciful now where he'd been unmerciful a moment before. Not good to drink while fighting. Dulled the senses. But he drank anyway, today, the one in his hand and each one the tender brought thenceforth in succession.

Later, the light late in the sky, the fighting began, and by then he was slobber drunk. He took his time and did not enter in for a great while. When he did, it was past midnight. A woman with large haunches and a plentiful bosom sat in the stairwell and sent out a bawdy tune. The noise of her filled the air. "Bulldaggers in the life!" she belted. "Honey, I have something to tell you, and it's worthwhile listenin' to. Put your little head on mah shoulder, so I can whisper to you." A mocking in her eye. He rose, slow-strolling to the center of the room. He remembered a blow to a man's jaw, a windpipe, a nose that flattened with a crunch beneath his fist. Someone stumbled and fell backward. His fists seemed heavy as sledgehammers. No one got up. Was it one man or many?

He demanded pay, then gave it straight to the tender before walking through the open door with his chest to the boardwalk. In the street he stood wavering. He untied his horse, mounted, and rode south.

Evelynne crouched near the slats in the alley. She watched him do his work, but when he left she came round the building into open ground. As he fled she called his name. When he turned to her, she caught a glimpse of his face, stricken and hard done.

He heeled his horse.

She held her arms across her chest, watching him go.

Finally she went home.

THIS TIME HIS flight sealed her from him. Her heart felt insufferably heavy. At the house she dismounted. Chan took the horses to the stable.

In her bedroom she sat in the dark at her vanity, dim light from the sky in the window. God of the wilderness, she thought, what is Nature to the ways of men? She had no more tears.

What welled in her breast was something she recognized before knowledge, even as a child. A quietness. Plaintive, lovely, an opening outward of beauty and affection. Here where she least expected it, she made the turn again, from no to yes.

She would not suffer her own fears, she told herself, nor the fear of any man. She certainly would not run after a man to turn him toward her. She kept her clothes on in bed, pulled the covering to her neck, and looked out the window into the blackness.

Love exists, only I am outside its sphere, she thought, barbing her insides until she slept.

41.

BELOW THE CITY Zion vomited from his horse before he wiped his mouth on his sleeve and kept on. His head pounded. Sweat greased his hairline. When at last he reached the mountains, he laid down his bedroll but made no fire. Over dry land cloud cover rolled, blotting out the sky. He heard rumblings from beyond the mountains. A cold wind came.

His depth of vision went to a singular blackness into which he peered, making out little until a branch of lightning fractured the heavens and sent a flash of light up from beneath the bowl of the earth. Darkness, followed by another flash in which the light carved peaks from the hollow of the night. Deep murmurs sounded, and thunder clapped overhead, loosening what hold the night had known. Water tumbled from the sky, flooding the land, making rivers of what lay below.

Cold to the bone, he pulled his hat down, letting the rain pummel him as lightning sang over the ridges and placed pitchforks on the sky. Through the slanted downpour he could see the face of a far-off mountain lit by fire. His father had spoken of the old times, likening the burning mountains to the gates of hell. His father had said it was 1910 when whole towns had burned, and every person in them. Billowing from Montana, Nevada, and Colorado, the aftermath had spread west to east, half the country engulfed in smoke.

When the rain stopped, the sky opened again.

At dawn he wandered farther east with the sun in his eyes until the light fell on his back. He wasn't sure if he might have killed a man at the Hungry Horse. He vowed he would not drink again and vowed also to forget Evelynne Lowry. He acknowledged how lonesome he was, sorrow in him like a shadow on the mountain.

CAMPING LIKE A vagabond outside Bozeman for half a year, he fought when he needed money. He wrestled steers for the jar and punch of feeling in his bones. His horse could run down steers. Middie manhandled them midstride. In high autumn he walked his horse down Main, bought a bath and shave, and went looking for work.

Make my way, he thought. God help me. Help me, for my mother.

He could read and write. She'd given him that. Quiet with people, he didn't show his hand. Nights as he rode on the mountain above Bozeman the words came to him from his mother and took hold again, the music seeming to rise out of him whenever he touched the memory: *When we who with unveiled faces are transformed.*

Poverty almost everywhere, he found only odd jobs.

He'd save his money, even if it took time. He'd work his way back to the Highline, buy back the family land, and be alone where it could do him good. He could abide people, he just couldn't abide the touch of a woman. The brokenness in him would need land and work and a great deal of time to mend.

The thought of years calmed him.

EVELYNNE AND BLACK KETTLE

42.

LATER, WHEN BLACK Kettle and Raymond made the circuit through Butte again Black Kettle heard from Evelynne in a most unexpected way. She approached him directly on the rodeo grounds with her retinue of Chinese and told him, "Do not speak with me again." She wore a red felt cloche hat and a yellow muslin dress with a merlot satin inlay. As she turned, Black Kettle's eyes followed her. She walked to the grandstand, where her father awaited her.

After the rodeo, when Raymond took the horses to water, an elderly Chinese man approached William on the boardwalk near the Lamar Hotel.

"Mr. Chan Wu," the man said, bowing.

"Black Kettle," said William.

"A letter for you, sir, from Miss Lowry." The man bowed again, a slight nod of the head, before he placed the envelope in William's hand and moved quickly away.

William turned the envelope over. The paper was thick, soft to the touch. He broke the seal and drew forth a letter of some length, written in a fine hand.

> *My Dear Mr. Black Kettle,*
>
> *I admire your horsemanship with all my heart. Having twice seen the speed and dexterity of your art with the horse and rope I am your debtor for the finest display of craft to have graced rodeo here in our great city.*
>
> *I don't relish public attention, and having spent recent years in my father's house due equally to the sorrow of great loss and by the wish to honor him, it has been long since I spoke much to a man other than him. Having great filial love for him as well as admiration for you and your horsemanship, I beg you to take leave of me and do not be seen with me again.*
>
> *In proportion to my love for horses and with reverence to the hand of the Almighty, I am proud to remain your obliged and faithful,*
>
> *Evelynne A. Lowry*

He held the letter high for a moment so the sun shone through. He felt taller. He sat on the boardwalk, placed the letter on his knees, and read her words again. A letter addressed to him. From her. He was still stunned when Raymond returned. He gave the letter to Raymond, who read it and frowned. They'd received the same education from the Sisters of God outside Lame Deer, women who avowed marriage to the Divine Presence and remained a mystery to him for how they loved so openly and set the white words in his mouth with confidence and conviction. They knew white men gave no quarter.

Raymond watched William.

"Black Kettle," Raymond said, "there's nothing for you here."

"I'll write her tonight and see," William replied.

Raymond went to tend his horse then, and William walked to his own horse. Taking two pheasants and a gray fox from the neck drape, he turned and strode directly to the mercantile, where he traded them for writing wares: ink and quill, stationery, and some few envelopes.

His letter, rendered on the flat of a hewn stump in a barren field, expressed his sentiment without reserve.

> *Dear Miss Lowry,*
> *I love your words with all my heart. ...*

THREE DAYS PASSED before he found means to deliver his missive. Above Butte, from a promontory hidden by trees, he saw the man Chan Wu enter town by wagon from the west. Mr. Wu halted, stepped down, and walked the boardwalk to the mercantile. William entered the city and waited near the corner of the store for Mr. Wu to emerge. When he did, William set his letter in the Chinese man's hand. "For the woman, Miss Lowry. Kindly for her."

"It is not possible for me to deliver this," Mr. Wu said. He tried to hand the letter back to Black Kettle. "You must go. You must not be seen."

Black Kettle refused. "Kindly, Mr. Wu," he said, "ask the woman if it's not possible."

43.

BLACK KETTLE RODE back to their makeshift camp above
the city, sheltered by aspen and a stand of white birch. A week
passed, and the two rarely spoke. There was a stillness to their
understanding. William walked in the trees among wild sunflowers, the brown-eyed blooms as big as a boy's hand. The fields
were filled with thumbnail-sized butterflies whose wings when
closed looked gray but in flight became bitter blue.

When at last Chan walked from the trees above their encampment, William was pleased at the man's bearing, a man not unlike him, at home in the forest.

Chan approached and bowed, palms up, a letter on the small
table his hands made. William thought he saw a smile in the
man's eye. "Thank you," said William, closing his eyes as he
lifted the letter to smell the envelope. Chan was already many
lengths along the path from which he'd come.

The letter filled William with delight.

> *Dear Mr. Black Kettle,*
> *I must be clear, I wish to cause my father no displeasure.*
> *He allows my letters without censure because his business is*
> *great and he does not suspect me lacking in reason enough to*
> *court disaster. I am as yet bound by a grief for which I have*
> *no voice, the loss of my beloved brother.*
> *Do not trifle with me. I know what I cannot bear.*
> *Write your letter and deliver it to Chan.*
> *He will come to you a day hence.*
> *Encourage our friendship, or release me.*
> *I await your words faithfully.*
> *Yours,*
> *Evelynne A. Lowry*

Black Kettle's response arrived precisely as requested.

> *Miss Lowry,*
> *Your affections, in friendship and for something higher, are*
> *a daring dream from which I assure you I will never wake. ...*

THE WAVE OF correspondence was steep. Chan delivered each letter faithfully, sometimes in bundles of two or three, a lightness to his step, and Evelynne's happiness steadily grew. William is so different from Zion, she thought. His words, in fact, might heal an unrequited heart. He was rodeoing all over Montana, but each time he passed through town, he'd find Chan and make the exchange. Still she forbade William to see her. But where Zion's mouth had been nearly empty, William's letters issued an infinite stream of vitality. Though Eve carried yet the barbs of the past, she tried to develop this new friendship openly.

After her brother's funeral Evelynne had gone to her room and lain fetal on her bed, covering her head in her arms. I led him to where his life was forfeit, she thought. The old dance visited her again. Her brother had said men found her beautiful. She felt unworthy. It broke her to think of him.

You will never marry. She heard her father's voice.

Yet each letter of William's answered one of hers.

Deep into their budding alliance, William pressed her:

> *Dear Miss Lowry,*
> *Come away with me. To me and my people. Let me come to you tomorrow. There is love for us beyond your father's reach.*
> *Yours,*
> *William*

SHE FELT AFRAID. His letter was too direct and she told him so.

> *Dear Mr. Black Kettle,*
> *I detest your letter.*
> *You assert yourself with little regard for my situation.*
> *First, nothing is beyond the reach of my father, I assure you.*
> *Second, when and if I have discussed love, it has been with the understanding of only friendship between us and nothing whatsoever to do with the bed of marriage to which you seem to beckon.*

*Too much too far, I say. You know this, as do I. You are a
son of your people.*

I am the daughter of a copper king.

*We are barred from one another. My father commands it,
and propriety forbids it. The loss of my father's only surviv-
ing relative, his sole daughter, would ruin him, as his death
would ruin me.*

*Your love is unwarranted, Mr. Black Kettle. I am not wor-
thy of it, nor can I return it.*

Do not call on me further.

I cannot love you.

Herewith, I stop our correspondence forever.

With regret,

Evelynne Lowry

Solemnly Chan presented the letter to William and retreated
up the mountain.

Black Kettle read Evelynne's pages, but what might have
daunted other men emboldened him.

44.

WILLIAM LAY ON his stomach, hidden on a rock promontory high over the movement of men and horses and machines. A very large city, Butte, the scurry of it like an anthill riled by a stick. In his hand he held a new letter to her, despite her last request that their correspondence stop. He saw Chan far below, the unmistakable forward slant of his gait. William traversed a rock chute on horseback and rode at a quick canter to the edge of the settlement, where he approached Chan from behind. Bringing his horse to a walk, he touched Chan's shoulder, then handed him the letter directly.

"Please," William said.

Chan nodded, his face like slate, putting the letter in the folds of his clothing.

The letter reestablished the exchange between Black Kettle and Evelynne, and the friendship commenced again.

Some weeks on, in early August, he declared his undying love once more. She needed a nudge, he thought. They were both of some age.

His letter tipped her over.

HER RETURN LETTER, dated August 15, 1931, was like a knife wound.

> Dearest William,
> Don't speak to me of conjugal love. Your letter sets me upon a desert with nothing but dread to guide me. I can't receive you as you would have me. Nor will I ever.
> I reject your proposal for my hand.
> I don't believe myself qualified. Love eludes me. I find myself plain. My father's hand covers my brother's mouth and sentences me. If I break from him, I break from all, and I endanger you. I will not do so.
> Release yourself from me now, while you may yet live.
> Do not write me. I dismiss you and Chan will not receive you.
> Evelynne

HE COULD HARDLY fathom her resistance.

He stared at the letter, looked to the ridgeline, and considered her.

That night he slept little, thinking perhaps she was right and he should go.

At dawn he resolved to convince her in person, though her father might kill him outright. An afternoon's journey to a meadow cradled among mountains cloaked in forest revealed the Lowrys' great house at the head of a long expanse. A structure of such size might harbor forty men, William thought, though he knew from her letters it housed only her and her father. The foreman, the hands, a retinue of Chinese men, and her personal attendant, Chan, slept in the outbuildings off the stables.

William remained hidden until nightfall. With Raymond he waited much of the night, then, with the moon low in the west, he left his horse high up the mountain, came through the forest to the meadow's edge, and stood peering at the house.

In one hand he held a rather large bouquet of wildflowers. In his vest pocket he kept the letter he'd written, a message composed of only one sentence: *Evelynne, come away with me*. He moved beneath the vaulted eaves of the veranda, stepping softly to the doors, where he performed the downward fall of the latch. The swing of the right door on oiled hinge left a slight opening through which he came to be inside. Foreign on the threshold, he took in the house at a glance.

He had never witnessed such opulence. He mounted the stairs quickly. On the upper floor one door was closed. The father. The other two doors were ajar, a knitting room he passed and her room, the scent of her like the faint taste of apples intermingled with grain. He held the flowers before him and walked in.

She lay under coverlet and quilt, a rich tapestry purple in the shadows, white lace at the fringe. On a white pillow her hair was like the wing of a blackbird, the texture and shine of blackness. He drew near and leaned over her, but she didn't wake. He stared at the pale glow of her face and the glint of red in her hair, full and lush in the dark, before he drew himself back. He left his letter on the bed stand near the glass bell of an oil lamp.

The flowers he placed on the coverlet in the nook her body made. He walked from the room, taking the stairs silently. He moved beyond the house into the forest, up the sweep of the mountain to his horse, and he and Raymond rode through the trees back toward the city. He thought of the vast spaces in that house and the separation between people, the distance one needed to cross to encounter another. As he lay down on his bedroll he watched the stars. He and Raymond sang together. The thought of her alone in that empty house saddened him.

45.

WHEN SHE WOKE, the gray predawn light lay steeped in the room. She breathed the scent of the flowers first, then saw them on the bed before her, the stalks gathered by a piece of calico, the blooms a torch of color. She touched the penstemon and bluebottle, feeling the dust of forest pollen on her fingertips. She knew he'd been here. As she lay with her head to the side, she could feel her heartbeat.

For a long while she did not rise but kept her gaze on the wildflowers. She was fearful. Her bedroom had been transgressed, but she herself had not been touched. She'd told him never to see or speak to her again. The gall of him coming here, scaling the stairs to her very room. As the sun came up she held the flowers in her hand. She lay still and thought of his courage. He risked his life by coming to her, and now the thought of his presence awakened a yearning to be something other than dutiful to her father.

Slowly her anger died away.

The sun was full in the room when she rose, noticing the letter for the first time on the bed stand.

To her own surprise, his boldness won the day.

CHAN CAME TO him on the mountain by nightfall to deliver her response, affirming her intentions and proposing a plan for when they might meet and fly away together.

Her discernment of her father's ways was nearly flawless. He loved rodeo and, above all, the skill and demand of team roping. She would request a private viewing of the best header and healer in Montana. Her father would not refuse her. In fact, the way she presented it, he took the idea as his own and made a great event of the endeavor.

"Who is it?" she questioned.

"The Indian boys," he answered. "No one else. Head and shoulders above the rest. The one named Black Kettle, his partner, Killsnight. I'll set up an arena right here in the lower field. Invite the brass. The governor, his lieutenants. All the dignitaries."

"Certainly," she said as he beamed at her.

The elopement, she thought, would be undetectable.

No more a recluse than I now, her father thought. He was glad for it. She'd been largely lost for some years. But since the horse and her return to society, he saw again how like her mother she could be.

"Handsome prize money to guarantee a performance to remember," he said.

"Certainly," she said.

He kissed her head. "Splendid, then. It shall be done."

The delight in his eye was infectious, ambition always his bed-fellow. She recognized that his will to see her under his roof and not another's was for the most part innocent. His motive toward men, Black Kettle and Killsnight among them, would not be.

But she had fallen now, making her heart the home of Black Kettle.

She thought of his eyes, darkly alive with light. His ebullience and the slender, broad-shouldered way of his movements among men. His letters, the blood-heart of his letters like the center of a wood lily. He had proven himself to her. She would make him prove nothing more.

The break man Zion came to mind for a moment, giving her a pang of sorrow, but she let it drift from her. Her letters to Black Kettle no longer hedged. She became explicit in her affections. The date was set for them to flee together, and she spoke plainly. Her desire had come to fruition, she would no longer quell the feeling.

Her final letter opened a door in Black Kettle. He found it difficult to keep himself from going to her in the days before they would be face to face. Mornings he left his horse to feed. Evenings he strode high into the mountains, where he stood on a stone ledge above the clouds. He watched the sky, a rim of moon in the west, the stars that rang with a clarity at once contained and infinite.

When word spread to the rodeo circuit of the Baron's desire to host William and Raymond at a given time and place, they entered Butte in answer to the Baron's call.

Soon, William thought, he and Evelynne and Raymond would return home together.

46.

FOR ALL WILLIAM'S love for Raymond, when they roped
and when they rode William held the world like a whistle to his
mouth while Raymond buried the world in the heart, a thorn
heavier than lead. Like brothers, they complemented one another in their friendship and the opposite symmetry of their bodies. In rodeos that ranged from Froid, Sidney, and Wolf Point
on the Highline south to Huntley Project and Billings and west
to Columbus, Big Timber, and Livingston along the mighty
Yellowstone River, the newspapers declared them the champi-
ons of Montana.

Earlier Evelynne and Chan had driven the wagon to town for
extra nails along with a few board feet of wood. The streets were
cluttered with the noise and stink of automobiles. "The end of
the horse, some say," said Chan.

"Never," she said. "A machine cannot imagine. In its properties
there is neither beauty nor intelligence." She smiled.

"Well said," said Chan, but she knew he did not agree. He fore-saw the landslide.

Let her father drive his Model Ts where he would, she thought, let him suture the world in rail ties. She would go by horse.

William and Raymond's invitation to a private roping exhibi-tion at the Baron's ranch included an award of one thousand dollars. She'd heard her father speak pompously. "To be split evenly!" he'd shouted. "Between the Indian Black Kettle and the Indian Killsnight in full warrior regalia!"

WHEN WILLIAM CAME to the roping grounds, he noted the newly laid fence, the open dirt field with a fresh set of gates, a center stock chute on the east end below the ranch house, and a wide corral at the back of the chute. The corral was stocked with steers that pushed against each other, lowing as they bumped shoulders and raised their thorny heads. The small, precise grandstand was already filling up with the dark-suited bodies of men, some few women in dignified gowns, and, next to the grandstand, a pole tent with a white canvas covering for shade. The mountains loomed behind.

A stair from the grandstand led to the ground, where there was an opening in the fence. The Baron had placed a man there so the circumference would be continuous to the horses and steers but the Baron could walk directly onto the rodeo grounds at his leisure.

When the copper king's daughter walked from the house to the grandstand William's face flushed, and he felt ashamed to have sold himself for this. His mouth was dry. He and Raymond wore fringed leggings and went bare-chested. They wore colored braid wraps, beaded moccasins, feathers in their hair. They'd painted their faces. He felt at once like a fighter and a child's doll. The small bandstand was set with boards still fresh from the cut. The men would drink and laugh and smoke cigars. Today they'd witness a roping display like none other, he thought. Tomorrow they would remember it not at all.

When he entered the gate at the east end and came into the arena with Killsnight to the applause of the crowd, Evelynne saw the hurt in his eyes, and she understood and reckoned the loss in him. Black Kettle and Killsnight rounded the far end before running the horses hard back down the middle. With a hand raised they sped out the east end, where they turned. The horses approached the open gates next to the cattle chute, prancing sideways until a cattleman who stood over the chute raised his hand and dropped a lever so the first steer was released.

The crowd exhaled as the horses bore down on the steer. The men in their abandon hovered as if in midair and let their ropes fly, William first, followed by Raymond. They took the steer flawlessly, spreading him horn to heel, and the same cycle was repeated to the delight of the crowd for a good while. Time and again Black Kettle hooked the horns as Killsnight whipped his arm in spirals overhead and released to rope the heels. They sent their lassoes over the hard gallop of the horses and the white-eyed rush of the steers while the animals were drawn taut and let go and the men trotted to the commencement gates, where they rode like thunder.

A handler on horseback at the back gate rounded each steer into another fenced circle offset to the west, where two more men opened and closed a holding corral. Each round had a hand-ful of steers. William kept the end of the rope tied hard and fast to the saddle horn. It took a gentle horse to keep from tripping the steer or breaking its legs by stopping too fast. The motion gave Raymond just the right turn to rope the back legs. The first time through they mishandled only one. The second round they mishandled none. But on the third things went haywire when a big almond-headed steer barreled out the chute, angled left, and beelined for the opening below the grandstand. As William tried to throw a rope on the animal, it cut in front of his horse, where the Baron's man waved frantically. The steer went straight on, horned him in the thigh, and trampled him before the beast flailed hooves and horns onto the stairs and barreled into the grandstand. Finally the animal lost its balance and fell sidelong to the ground, scrambling to all fours again as it glanced off the corner of the grandstand and passed through the pole tent, fran-tic-eyed. The steer knocked over a few tables, then ran bawling toward a stand of pines.

People craned their necks as the animal moved through the trees and went up the mountain, where it was lost to sight. They all seemed to murmur at once.

"Okay, now, everyone," the Baron lifted his voice. "Animals will be animals. Won't happen again," he said. "Go ahead and be seated." He called to his man below, who was up off the ground now. The man had leaned himself slowly back into position at the opening. His pants were torn at the left thigh, the flesh split open, a swatch of blood visible below the tear line. "You all right there?" the Baron said.

"Yes, sir," the man answered, staring out to the rodeo grounds.

The Baron walked down the steps. "Shoot the next one in the head tries to do that again," the Baron said.

"Yes, sir," the man said.

Josef Lowry waved Black Kettle and Killsnight to the opening. They brought their horses up in front of the grandstand, where the animals breathed heavily.

"Change of plan," the Baron said, loud-lipped, as if spitting the words from his mouth. His face bloomed red. "Eight head of steers left in that pen. You don't rope every one of them clean, you don't get the prize money, you hear?" He waved his hand back to the people in the stands. "Hired you to do a job, now do it."

The crowd shuffled. A man catcalled.

Black Kettle and Killsnight proceeded to rope every last steer without a hitch. Not one neck-rope, half-head, or single-leg catch. Straight double-horn, double-leg. When it was done the people stood cheering as the Baron smiled wide in their midst. He shouted with delight and waved the riders over. When they sat astride their horses before the standing crowd, the Baron, with a booming voice, said, "I give you Black Kettle and Killsnight, header and heeler extraordinaire!" Wildly clapping their hands, the people shouted their approval. The two men were stoic as the crowd applauded. In total they'd roped twenty-six head. The horses were weary. The Baron gestured to the ropers, and they rode out the east gate of the arena to wait for him.

EVELYNNE FOLLOWED HER father around to where Black Kettle and Killsnight had dismounted. The Cheyenne horses stood behind the riders.

Her father approached the men directly and placed four one-hundred-dollar bills in each man's hand along with a canvas pouch containing one hundred silver dollars. The men received the money without a word. The people had fled the grandstand entirely and appeared to frolic in the shade of the pole tent. Evelynne glanced over her shoulder once before she nodded to Raymond, stepped forward, and put out her hand toward William.

"Heartfelt congratulations," she said.

He took her hand without speaking.

Her father stepped between them, saying to Black Kettle, "You can go now." To his daughter he gave a sharp look.

She ignored him, stepped around, and placed her hand on William's arm.

"I will have my say, Father," she said, and her father appeared dumbfounded. "Go on," she said, waving him off. He stared at her for a moment, grimaced, and turned from her, grunting his disapproval all the way to the pole tent. He entered the mingle of the guests. Still with half an eye on her, he righted an overturned table, filled his glass, and threw back plugs of whiskey. Slow down, he told himself. Let her be. But the boil in him would not be quieted.

47.

"YOU'RE VERY SKILLED," she said to Black Kettle and Killsnight. When Black Kettle looked into her eyes, she drew near, whispering, "I remember how foolish you were to come to me when we first met."

"Foolish?" he questioned.

Raymond took the horses and walked a distance away.

"Foolish," she said. He gazed at her lips when she spoke. "But also brave."

"Is it brave to speak to a woman?" he asked. Her eyes were a flourish of color, dark and green, he thought, like the forests in these loyal mountains.

"No," she said. "It's brave for any man to speak to Josef Lowry's daughter."

"I would speak to you forever," he said.

"We risk my father's wrath."

Black Kettle took her hand in both of his. "We risk what must be risked."

She looked over her shoulder, and when she turned back to him, her eyes were pained. Her father advanced toward them. His stride harbored hatred. As Josef Lowry gave a sharp call, a shout hardly contained, William stiffened and let go of her hand. In a moment the Baron was upon them.

"Leave," he said sternly to Black Kettle.

"Sir?" said Black Kettle, his blood rising as he stared into the Baron's eyes.

"You offend me," Josef Lowry said. "Take your leave now." The Baron's head was hatless. Thin silver hair swept back from a sharp widow's peak, the skin crimson as if wounded at the hairline.

Black Kettle did not look away.

Josef took Evelynne's shoulders then, tucking her into his arm. She tried to speak, but he gripped her harshly. "With me!" he said, moving her briskly toward the house. Twisting her shoulders, she broke his grip but kept walking.

Black Kettle turned on the heel of his boot and went to his horse. He'd seen the face of the man. A look that would have him and Lowry killing each other if he did not leave now. He walked straight to Raymond and took the reins. Lowry walked the slight incline to the house with Evelynne. He pushed Evelynne inside, then paused in the doorway to eye Black Kettle with contempt before he abruptly closed the doors behind him.

Black Kettle watched Raymond, then looked at the sky. The day turns, he thought. I must turn it back before it's too late.

A foreman came round the side of the house. He wore spurs and a wide, straight mustache greased to long points, the red gash of his mouth thin-lipped and hard. He went directly to the crowd and dismissed them. They took their time clearing, but the foreman pressed them along to the horses, a handful of carriages, and the Model Ts. The men muttered as they went. "No way to treat a guest!" "Give a man a drink and run him off. What's this Lowry?" The women marched in front, their bodies inflexible and faces pinched.

Raymond took mount. "We must go, William."

The group passed before them. Raymond and Black Kettle saw a funnel of ire in the face of the foreman, who gave a last angry push to move the crowd on.

When he turned, staring back through the trees with his hand on his holster, Raymond hissed, "Get on your horse now, Black Kettle."

As William mounted, Josef Lowry came from the house and fired a double-barreled shotgun over their heads.

William and Raymond jerked the horses hard, riding low in the saddle into the forest. From the side two men came on, pointing guns while William and Raymond hard-heeled the animals. They sped north away from Lowry and his men and climbed the entire treed hill until they dropped behind the first ridge, where they halted for a moment, listening.

A rifle shot rang out. They heard no other horses.

William leapt to the ground to run back to the ridgeline. He lay on his belly and peered down to the clearing. There Lowry walked with the foreman, guns in hand, searching the ridge with their eyes. The two other men stood behind them. Black

Kettle held still. Lowry bumped the butt of his gun to the foreman's shoulder. The two seemed to laugh, a sound unclear from William's vantage.

Raymond came up beside him.

"We must go," Raymond whispered.

William put his hand over Raymond's mouth. "I must stay," he said.

48.

FOR A SECOND time William Black Kettle entered the house of the copper king and mounted the stairs. The top of his head felt afire. Halting, he knelt, pressing his hands to the wood as he peered into the dark. The possibility of violent ambush lay beyond, here in the upper rooms, he thought. Lowry in the dark behind the barrel of a gun. But he saw no one, and no sound came. Moving with great stealth, he entered Evelynne's room, placed his hand over her mouth, and hushed her.

"With me," he whispered sharply, "away!" When she rose, her form flowed around him and he felt crushed by the intimacy of her presence. She went to the wardrobe, drew a long skirt over her nightclothes, and tied the skirt at her waist. Turning from him she pulled her stockings to midthigh. His eyes darted from the window to the door and back to her.

She set a black woolen coat around her shoulders, carried her boots in her hands, and went to him. "Go," she whispered as she touched his shoulder. Her face was like marble, her hands open.

They came from her room, and he paused.

"Wait." He walked directly to the room of her father, entered, and positioned himself in the dark by the bed. Evelynne stood in the doorway behind him. She wanted to draw Black Kettle out of the room as one might draw breath.

Josef Lowry was encased in blankets.

A whiskey bottle stood on the bed stand. William saw an overturned glass, a liquor spill. The Baron faced away from him, his breathing a thick, low drone.

Standing over him, William knew no fear.

An enemy kills an enemy, he thought, and yet here the copper man sleeps. No threat at all.

He would have me as an enemy, but we are not enemies. Still, the war in us beckons, William thought, and so he stepped forward, touching the bridge of Lowry's nose. As William counted coup, the copper king started, and William lifted his hand away. Lowry exhaled heavily then before the hum of his breathing returned to itself. Black Kettle turned, taking Evelynne's hand so she followed him down the stairs to the front doors. She halted, and they kissed one another fiercely before she looked up at William.

"Come away," he said.

"Not yet," she whispered, touching his face.

He stared at her.

"You placed your hand on my father's head," she said.

"It is between him and me," Black Kettle replied.

"If he discovers us, he will surely kill you," she said. "He'll chain me to this house, and he'll take your life."

Black Kettle looked hard on her.

"I am not easily destroyed," he said.

"We can't go now," she said. "We must be wise!"

"If we leave now, this is wisdom," he said. "Raymond is a mile up the mountain. He waits for us. You're not safe in your father's house."

"No, I am safe," she said. She gripped his arms. She pressed her fingers to his lips. "My father reaches all of Montana, even to the great cities of the east. When I leave, it must be without his knowing when or where or with whom. We'll wait. For our peace, we need his blindness."

She lifted his hands, kissing them.

"How, then?" he asked, a breath of vapor from his mouth.

"Meet me at Turner's Crossing. In one week."

She touched his shoulder. "He'll drink now for some days. After everything today he'll gloat. He'll binge, oblivious of what passes between you and me. Then, when he no longer thinks of you, we'll leave together. That way we'll be safe until we reach your people. When he discovers it, he'll brew over the loss. He'll want to cause you great harm. But I can assuage him once we're far away and he doesn't know where I've gone."

William held her face. He saw the rightness of her way. "Yes," he said. "I will meet you." Her hair was tied loosely with a black satin ribbon. Drawing her close, he breathed the scent of her

skin. She untied the ribbon and gave it to him. Her hair fell full
on her shoulders.

She watched the darkness at the top of the staircase.

He took her fingers and blew heat into them.

"Go," she said as she arched into his embrace.

49.

HE SHOULD HAVE stayed to stake his claim in the mountains, but he decided to ride a day or two out with Raymond to secure the initial stage of Raymond's passage. Then he would return to meet Evelynne at the crossing.

IN THE MORNING, when he and Killsnight rode the trail east beyond the city, a gang of men emerged from the trees. The foreman with the barbed mustache led them.

Black Kettle and Killsnight set their horses to flight. The chase sent them along a gulley before they spilled onto open ground, where they split paths, William going north and Raymond south. The gang followed Raymond while William topped a ridge, galloping among pine and ash, then turning back until he pulled up on a second, less lofty ridge. The chase came to an end with Raymond overtaken by horsemen who dragged him from his horse and set about beating him with the butts of their rifles. They will kill him, Black Kettle thought as he sped down the ridgeline. He flew through an opening in the trees into the gap of grass and young growth, where he sent his horse into the fray, yelling, *"Hokahey! Hokahey!* We are like the sun! We will never die!"

He and Raymond were pummeled near to death, their clothes removed, all their belongings taken. Their horses were sent bolting into the forest.

When William emerged from the dark of his dreams, the foreman knelt over him.

"Did you think this money was yours to keep?" he said quietly, his mouth near William's cheekbone. His breath stank. He held the fresh bills, the bags of silver. He rose and placed the money in his saddlebags. The clothes and blankets the foreman rolled together, dousing them with liquor from a flask. He set a match to them, the fire burning red and black as smoke billowed from the flame.

Returning, the man came to one knee and drew near to William's ear.

"The money was never yours," he said. He tapped William's face with his boot then before walking to where he straddled Raymond. Killsnight lay face down, unmoving. "Because of Josef Lowry you have your life. Take it and leave this place." He kicked Raymond's ribs.

"Lady Luck," the foreman said, shaking his head. "She's with you today." He mounted his horse, and the gang of men followed, leaving William and Raymond naked on the ground. Busted and bruised, pressed down upon rock and white grass,

William said nothing but watched as Raymond opened his blotted eyes and breathed.

They heard the wind and at last the crunch of pine needles and finally William saw the horses' slender faces hidden among the trees, Raymond's bluish sable mare and William's black-and-white paint. He made a clicking sound, and the horse moved alongside him. He lay against the horse's neck before he put his fists in its mane and managed to pull himself over the back and let his body rest. Raymond did the same.

"Home," William said. The horses went forward, entering the mountains north. Far on William and Raymond drank water from a creekbed and were revived. They took a few ragged clothes from the line outside a farmhouse and went on through days and nights along paths obscure to men until at last they entered the Tongue River country of the Cheyenne, where they were met by hands that carried them whole to the bosom of their mothers who prayed over them, and caressed them.

50.

AT THE APPOINTED time, Evelynne Lowry came to Turner's Crossing with only the garments she wore, her riding breeches under her long dress, the coat of a man, her black short hat, and the horse she rode. She waited all day and kept her vigil into the dark, but Black Kettle did not appear. She made no fire. The night was cold. She sat astride her horse, looking to the stars. A field of light spread overhead, unfathomable in the far darkness, and yet the light burnished the coat on her horse's neck and touched her hand.

The mosaic of the sky, inbreathed with stars, devastated her. Truth whole demands more than one is able to give. Truth bleeds you, she thought, more than is warranted, more than a body can endure.

She waited through the next day. William wasn't coming, she knew that now.

Despairing, she rode back to the ranch house.

She went to Chan, asking him to inquire discreetely.

He consulted her father's men and found deceit.

Josef Lowry had planned from the beginning to give Killsnight and Black Kettle the money, then ambush them and take it back. Beat them, then send them away.

Evelynne felt a fire in her to consume the world.

Outside the ranch house she nearly shouted at Chan. "Why do men act like fools?"

He turned from her, watching the mountains.

She'd been rash.

"Please," she said more softly.

He was quiet a long while before he turned to her again.

"The railroads reached two hundred thousand miles of track before World War I," he said. "Three hundred thousand a decade later. Four hundred thousand by 1930. On the backs of my countrymen your country is born."

"My country?" she said, placing her hand on Chan's arm. "Our country. Yours and mine."

Chan didn't speak.

She stared into his face.

"Whose country stands by as its people collapse?" he asked. "Whose country abuses the Chinese, the Indian, the black man, even the poor white, and gives only to the rich white? Whose country binds me to this place?"

"This country," she said plainly. "To my shame."

"To our shame," he said. "To the shame of us all. America forsakes her own."

She had been willing to flee, but she saw now that he too desired a life apart from the Baron. "I'm sorry," she said.

"It's nothing," he replied, but when he moved away from her, she saw him check his emotion. He walked down through the field. She followed him through the slight draw out onto the grass beside the arena, where he went to the stables and she walked toward the forest, feeling undone. When she returned to the house, she found her father unconscious in his leather reading chair. She admitted now that she had some of her father's disregard for others, but she was also isolated, incapable of helping herself or Chan. She put her face in her hands. Abruptly she approached and stood over her father and considered doing him violence.

She extended her hand over his face. Her body shook.

She retreated to her bedroom, where she stayed.

1932

51.

MUCH TIME WOULD pass before Black Kettle and Killsnight healed.

Darker and deeper the shadow in Killsnight.

But Black Kettle still held hope for peace. He wanted to write Evelynne, to explain, but the thought of her waiting for him and finding nothing subdued him. He could not return to her bruised and broken. He knew he must bide his time. Surely her father watched the post. He could not be found out by writing her. The Great Spirit would move and the seasons change. He vowed to see her when he was fully healed, and be married to her forever.

His people would make him whole. Then he would go to her.

Raymond Killsnight

52.

At last william and Raymond recovered from their wounds. Raymond carried in his bone and blood hatred for the white man, hate like a cataract over the eyes. But William, desiring Evelynne, maintained a place of calm inside himself.

When spring came he thought roping might draw Raymond back to what he'd been. So it came to be on a day hot with sun they set out together for a rodeo in Mizpah. He'd been through that high country with Raymond before, across Hell Roaring Plateau and west to Two Oceans, where the water divided, going west to the Pacific or east to the Atlantic. The rodeo in Mizpah was like most, hard riding and filled with ranch hands, where women gathered with men as children ran the outskirts trying to mimic the feats of the cowboys. There was only one bar in Mizpah, the Steerhorn.

William and Raymond won the team roping handily.

To his delight, William saw the big man Middie again. He'd won the steer wrestling, and afterward they stood together in the shade of a cottonwood near the rodeo grounds, where they made plans to share a fire that night before moving on.

When they parted, William tended to his horse as Middie went to town. Later, when Raymond started to walk toward Mizpah too, William felt unsettled.

William needed only his share of the purse along with a few more of the same size to retrieve Evelynne by train, giving her passage this time not merely by horse but iron horse and with money for the dining car. He knew the image of them together sharing passage on a train would sorely wound white sensibilities. Still he clung to it, and if not them together, then separately, an arrangement in which he'd ride in the car behind her until Billings, where they would disembark and meet each other along the trail toward Lame Deer.

He wanted Raymond to make camp with him outside town, waiting for Middie, but Raymond refused with a dark build in his eyes, saying, "I'll do what I want and meet you when I'm done." He gestured with his chin, signaling he'd have a drink in town.

"Don't," Black Kettle said, but Raymond ignored him, leaving Black Kettle no choice but to follow.

The bar had an oval of dark wood in the back, where men gathered, shouting. Raymond and William walked in unnoticed. Wagers were slammed on the counter, and loud voices came from raucous mouths as the two friends watched until the tender, a chunk of a man with thick arms and legs, banged a shotgun on the counter. The men cussed him, but everyone went quiet. "He'll be here in a goddamned minute!" he yelled. "Shut your thorny traps."

A man grumbled, but the tender jerked toward him, pointing the weapon over the man's shoulder. "Shut your pie hole!" he said. "He'll be here. Half monster, half man. Hold your hats and let me tally the bets."

The men laughed as the tender's toothless grin split his face in two. His daughters, two big middle-aged women, ran the bar as he moved among the men. "We gotta get your bets down kindly like so we can pay up when the winning's done. We have our lineup. Watch out. He's got a fist is like the kick of a mule."

When Middie walked in the back door, William smiled before he and Raymond sat down at a table against the wall to watch.

"Here he is now!" the tender said. "The barn burner! The one I got all my bets on. Not one of you is beatin' the house tonight." He beamed. The men slapped their hands on each other's backs. They were far into the liquor. The tender handed Middie a tumbler of whiskey, and Middie threw it back, feeling the bite of the alcohol at the back of his throat. He walked to the middle of the hardwood floor and waited. His denim shirt was frayed at the cuffs and collar, but he wore new blue jeans. When Middie saw the two Indians, he nodded to them.

Under the sway of drink people leered at him like crazed fools. A man in the crowd called out, "After him, Swede!" And Swede, far older than Middie, took off his shirt and came in bare-chested with his elbows down, his knuckles curled back. The challenger snapped a jab out in front of him, shaking his arms as he approached on a straight march. In the end he threw no punch at all but bullrushed Middie, and Middie let the man's head hit his stomach before he placed a hand on Swede's chin, slamming his elbow into the crease between the man's shoulder and his ear. When Swede fell to his knees, Middie loosed his jaw with a blow that sounded like it issued from a forge. The man crumpled to the floor while the others jeered.

The next fighter emerged, grim-faced, with black hair shorn as if with a longknife. The crowd moved in as he danced toward Middie and lunged finally, trying to take out a leg. Middie corralled the man at the waist, lifting him overhead before he threw him on the ground. The body bounced once, then rolled over, the eyes locked back in the skull.

The room went silent before it erupted.

The tender moved like a spider, collecting money.

When the rush of the fights subsided, William and Raymond approached the counter and Middie joined them.

William congratulated him on the fighting.

The tender stood with wet lower lip extended, dumbfounded as he watched the exchange. Two Injuns right here in my tavern, he thought. I'll be a son of a bitch.

"Drinks," Killsnight said.

"Th' hell if I serve you," the tender said, screwing up his face.

Raymond's face coiled at the tender, who glared back and chewed his cheek.

"Drinks!" Raymond shouted, but now everyone turned.

The tender's lip curled.

"Don't serve your kind," he said. "No one does."

Middie leaned into the barman's face. "Serve them your best

whiskey," he said. He lifted his jaw to William and Raymond. "Two whiskeys."

The tender pointed his nose at the girls, and they filled two shots. Raymond drank his down, and William lifted his to Middie, smiled, and drank it through. They placed coins on the table next to the empty glasses.

Heavy-lidded, the men trained their gaze on Black Kettle and Killsnight. Malice emanated from their eyes. The air was thick with heat along with the tangy smell of men and breath, the odors of body and hair and clothing unwashed for days.

"Many thanks," said William as he turned to Middie. "Time we go now." He took Raymond's arm, leading him toward the short hall out the back of the bar.

Middie heard the spring on the back screen, then heard the door slap closed. He was glad for having shut the bartender's mouth. "Good for it," he told the tender as he nodded to the coins. Middie liked it fair. "They paid good money."

The tender nodded, but his face looked blistered.

Eyes like a skunk cave, Middie thought as the tender handed him his fight money. Middie made his way through the men to the front. He came out into late sun and wondered where the two Indians had gone as he walked the slim boardwalk past the post office onto the dirt.

He heard a distant shout and turned in the direction of the sound.

More words came. "Hey, Injun!"

"White pig," was the response.

"Shut your jaw, boy."

As Middie rounded the corner of the post office he saw a man in coveralls, wet-mouthed drunk. Black Kettle and Killsnight stood before him.

"This ain't no red-man town," the man said, lurching forward to grasp at Killsnight's neck. William put his hand in front of the man's face. But the drunk flared as he shoved William's hand away and tried to lock Raymond's neck in the crook of his arm.

Raymond slipped the man's hold and moved laterally. The man crouched, and when he drew a pistol from his boot, Raymond kicked him hard in the side, causing him to fall over. The man came to one knee and brought the pistol around as William shouted and Raymond charged, punching the man's face so hard he went to both knees again and the pistol came free.

The farmer scrambled for it, but Raymond snatched it up, put it to the man's skull and fired.

The head nodded hard to the side. The man slumped, and his butt came to rest on his heels. He didn't move. The small hole on one side of his head carved a divot the size of a soup ladle on the other. A spray of crimson colored the dirt. The farmer sat like a penitent now, his torso upright, his knees embedded in earth, his head sloped to the side and mouth open as if in a cry.

Middie stepped forward.

Raymond and William stared at the dead man.

The back screen of the bar swung wide, and three men came into the clear.

Raymond dropped the gun.

"Run," Middie said.

William and Raymond bolted, and the white men's faces

seemed to break open as Middie strode toward them, saying in a loud voice, "Stay where you are!"

But they shouted like madmen and came on.

Middie met the first one with a fist that laid the man backward. He tripped the second and sent him sprawling. The third got through, but Middie ran him down, shouldering him through some fencing into a muddied circumference where an old horse stood. Middie walked back to the dead man, who still knelt with his hands on his knees. A small crowd began to gather, a band of men and some few women. "No use goin' after them," Middie said. "Enough blood for today." The crowd gaped at the scene. Their faces were black with rage.

"Had it comin'," Middie said. "Dead man tried to shoot someone."

Middie nodded as he walked through them into the gap between the post office and the broken corral. He retrieved his horse from in front of the saloon. Black Kettle and Killsnight needed his help now. A mob would form behind the buildings. The men of Mizpah would seek the Cheyenne to kill them. He went south in the direction he thought the two might go, south and east to Crow Agency and Busby, Lame Deer and Tongue River country.

53.

RAYMOND WAS HIDDEN by William and a small band of Cheyenne in the clay hills near Busby.

From Mizpah a troupe of men rode on to the courthouse in Billings, where the judge would hear nothing of the case but sent them on to what remained of the military tribunal at Fort Keogh in Miles City. There they gained slipshod audience from a retired colonel who lived in the wake of the give-over of Fort Keogh to the US Department of Agriculture.

"Hot summer," he said, "hottest day on record about a week ago. One hundred seventeen degrees." Thin and Nordic-white with near orange hair, he stood on the porch of an outbuilding and squinted at the men. "Best get shade," he said. "Down by the river. Cool those horses down." They left him, at last making payment to a federal marshal, a man with a habit of imbibing the still whiskey of those who during prohibition he was tasked to put in jail but who were his friends and who remained his source of drink. Like their own Mizpah, in Miles City liquor had boomed. Nearly everywhere inside the four lines of Montana the end of prohibition had generated an outbreak of liquor lust.

The men and the marshal drank together.

"Reckon we ought to make things right," the marshal said. He was a small man with bony arms and a small paunch. He kicked his boots up on the edge of a round table.

"Yes," the men responded.

"Need to string that boy up," said a red-bearded man with glazed eyes.

"Payment for deeds done," said another.

54.

MIDDIE MADE IT to the Cheyenne at Tongue River, where he was vouched for by William. He bore gifts of deer and muskrat as well as the hide of a bear.

Not long after his arrival two men stole into the Cheyenne encampment and took away a small boy while everyone was sleeping.

They threatened to cut out his tongue unless he told them the whereabouts of Killsnight. The boy's eyes darted from man to man as they cuffed him about the shoulders, brandishing their knives.

When the boy spoke, they discarded him and rode away.

By the time the boy made it back to alert the camp, the men had all the jump they needed. No good would come of a war party. Raymond's mother approached William. "Take this," she said, handing him Bull Killsnight's war club. Then William and

Middie rode with abandon to intersect a trail not hard to follow, the white men's horses having left a channel of indentations.

The path led from the sand cliffs off toward Miles City, and when at last they approached the low hills of the town, Middie convinced William to stay hidden. The Yellowstone River broke away east. They would need to use surprise.

"They'll take you too," said Middie. "Remain here. I'll seek Raymond first and return with word. Then we'll plan together how to free him."

William agreed, watching from a slight rise in the land, his horse in the coulee behind him as Middie skirted the town and disappeared finally among the buildings. He came to the court-house and went inside. The clerk had no word. He asked a man walking the boardwalk, who stared at him, dumb-faced. He rode toward the main store, then the fort.

William waited but saw nothing. Finally he retrieved his horse and descended by cover of tree and gulley. Turning south, he took up the club Killsnight's mother had given him, laying it across his lap as he came into the open, riding directly down Main Street. He did not look right or left. Onlookers eyed him with a squint and side glance. He rode past the edge of town where he spotted Middie again. They approached a dry creek bottom from oppo-site directions but came at the same time upon the tree from which Raymond Killsnight's body hung.

Black Kettle stood in the saddle, his vision narrowed to a point.

Raymond's body, dark in the sky, turned slightly in the wind. Black Kettle lifted the club in his right hand. A piercing scream erupted from his throat. With fist and heel he turned his horse, making the animal fly straight for the town. In the scabbard the butt of his rifle bumped his thigh as he gripped the mane with his free hand.

He will bear their blood away, Middie thought, and they will kill him.

Middie heeled his horse as the animal torqued its neck, jumping forward over the plain. A foreboding struck him, a knife of hatred for his own. He'd put a stop to all this, he thought. He'd carry Black Kettle away. The image of Killsnight's turned neck and slack body sickened him. He pounded the shoulders of his horse and cursed God and man.

A small mob gathered at the opposite end of town as Black Kettle lay low in the mount, running his horse through the trees. Just as he turned the horse directly at the hangmen, Middie came alongside, the two at a full gallop. Middie leapt to William's back, hauling him to the ground. He knocked William unconscious with a blow to the side of the head. Bullets hit the dirt around them, but Middie hoisted Black Kettle's limp body to his lap atop the horse. Trailing Black Kettle's mount behind, he banked away from the gunfire, winding swiftly into a near coulee before he came out at last onto the plain. He galloped hard for a great while with no sound but the horses and the wind.

Eventually he met the basin of the Bighorn in the space between the Powder and Tongue rivers. Into the darkness he rode, returning Black Kettle to the lodge of his parents, to his people, where Middie crouched and told them what had become of Killsnight and what awaited their son in Miles City should he seek the revenge that was his due.

THAT NIGHT WILLIAM woke in the arms of his father and struggled against him. But his father held him down, placing his hand on his son's chest. "Be still," his father said. "No more killing."

"Let me go," William said.

"We need our sons," his father said. "You will stay." He kept his hand on William's chest, watching the hatred fill his son's eyes, then subside. In the dark the tribe heard the cries of Killsnight's mother while William lay still in his father's arms. In the end William went silent and stared into the blackness.

55.

MIDDIE REMAINED WITH the Tongue River Cheyenne for a time.

Largely silent among them, he was of some help as he roamed the land to find game. He returned carrying a crown buck in his arms, a doe, or a string of pheasants. He set these at the openings of the lodges, where a quiet had fallen after much wailing and cutting of hair and tearing of clothes.

Mending would be long in coming, he thought.

There are only two races of men, he told himself. Decent and unprincipled.

In the lodge of Black Kettle he saw the deep cuts on William's skin. His head of hair shorn. He lay in a bed of buffalo robes, his eyes sunk to a far darkness.

Middie watched over William as his wounds slowly began to heal, ridges of skin like pale furrows on his arms and chest, the eyes still hidden in the chamber of his face, forsaken.

The Baron

56.

In the great chair the copper king, Josef Lowry, sat with an unlit cigar in his mouth. His hands rested on leather armrests. His fingers touched copper buttons that pinned leather to wood. He loved his daughter, but it was ever more apparent that she had no love for his ideas. He'd railed against her, cornered her, and succeeded, he thought, in subduing her. But she was not easily subdued. Why did he do that? he asked himself. In the end she seemed to give in just to humor him, letting him drone on as she went somewhere inside herself.

Perhaps he didn't love her at all, perhaps he had never loved his daughter, or his son either, but simply used them as a stopper for his own grief. When her mother had died, he'd closed himself against others. He had his empire now. His wife and son were dead. The great window of his house in the city opened upon the valley. He looked over the underground mines that circumscribed his land and undercut the land of his competitors.

His mind whirred with the work of men and machines. If he could, he'd make an entire house of buffed and gleaming copper. He knew Eve was in the other room, likely dark again over how he'd tried to obliterate her. It is better this way, he told himself. She needed him. She would carry on and own this land, the mountains of copper, the millions. Everything.

A cat lay sleeping in his lap, brown and beautiful in the face. Another, a smoky Russian, walked and purred and brushed against the Baron's shin. The black Russian was his favorite. The cat's supple movements reminded him of Evelynne's mother when the young family and love had been laid out before them like an invitation. He had grave thoughts now. Anymore only drink could turn him, Evelynne's presence a sharp reminder of his unfaithfulness and the whoring he'd partaken of in his years of sorrow. Admittedly after his wife's death he'd faltered.

He hated the memories.

He'd brought Evelynne to the city house after the rodeo debacle at the ranch. Men are uncouth, he thought. Here she is safe. But since the exhibition, she seemed to have gone half mad.

This much he knew: the world was no place for a woman. He wouldn't put it past any man to try to take her away from him to gain a share of the plunder. He picked up the decanter of cognac, filled the glass again, and raised it to his lips. In his swarthy hand the liquor looked charcoal. He needed to make her stay here in the city when he was away. He thought he might have to start locking her in her bedroom. She'd hate him for it, but her own good was a treasure he would not relinquish.

57.

SHE SAW THE black cat where it lay on the hardwood, big
Russian paws pushed to the wainscoted wall. The cat appeared
boneless, lost in everlasting sleep. Evelynne wished for a sense
of peace herself, but holding her father's silver-plated Colt in her
hand, she knew the night would be cold and she'd need to take
her father's coat and the rifle too, not just the .45. She would take
none of her father's money. He'd miss his belongings and hate
her, not for what she took but for leaving.

How could he not know, after all that had gone on, that she
needed life away from him and the possibility of her own family?
She wanted her face to the wind without his callused hand holding her back. She had heard nothing from Black Kettle. She'd
go to him herself, she thought, and see what needed to be seen.
She'd leave tonight. She would wait no longer.

She rose and put the gun down on the countertop, opening the
drawer where he kept her mother's crucifix. Beneath the crucifix

lay a sepia photograph of him, his face both ashen and bold as he stood on Butte Hill with the sky behind him, his hands on his hips, one boot up on a nearby rock. She slid the photograph free and placed it under the gun and looked back in the drawer at the crucifix. Like an object of living bone, the image seemed wedded to her. She sometimes saw herself as wedded to suffering. Married to God, she thought, and remembered the nuns at the small church off Front Street: Our Lady of the Rockies. Her father dined with them the first Friday of each month. Evelynne often joined him. The crucifix was made of cream-white ivory, the body on the cross stained brown at the nail holes. She brought the cross to her mouth and kissed the lips of Christ.

The days had lain heavy on her, and she'd sensed something larger than winter enfolding her. She would need to go forward without regard for her father's goodwill.

She moved her hand into the waistband of her skirt and placed the crucifix under her girdle against her hip bone. She left the kitchen and passed through the great room, where her father sat in his big-armed chair. He stared distantly out the front window.

She went to her room.

On toward evening, still he hadn't moved. At long last he fell asleep. She waited until his breathing was heavy.

Robed in her father's long coat and her riding clothes, she donned his hat in the kitchen, placing the pistol in the left pocket of the coat, his photograph in the right.

She closed the back door behind her.

She went into the street and walked. She'd stuffed the coat's shoulders and sleeves and turned the front of his hat down to cover her face. Everyone knew her here. In the folds of the coat she carried the rifle. She kept to the back streets. The night was black, the air not unbearably cold.

Chan met her at the east road near the edge of the aspen grove. He had his own horse and hers. Surely her father would not begrudge her Imber. The horse bore on his haunches a large bundle of her clothing wrapped in tarp, with three books secreted inside. Dickinson, Whitman, Hopkins.

She embraced Chan and took mount. They pointed the horses west. Rifle in the scabbard, she took the pistol from the front left pocket of the coat and tucked it into the waistband of her riding pants. As they moved down through the aspen grove the leaves winked silver in the darkness. She leaned forward, placing her chest and neck on the neck of the horse. She removed her glove, moving her hand down the jawline until the horse craned its neck and she put her hand under his muzzle and fed him a lump of sugar. Imber nodded. Riding on, Evelynne rose in the saddle, the warmth of the horse's mouth a remnant in the palm of her hand. They were already more than a mile from town, the path open, the snow a thin blanket in the fields. Her heart drummed in her throat. In the early dark the horse moved beneath her like a river.

A FEW DAYS later she and Chan halted in the cottonwoods along the Yellowstone outside Billings. They dismounted and made a light breakfast of coffee with biscuits and bacon. Chan would escape the Baron through Nevada to San Francisco along a chain of relatives that led to California and finally Chinatown. Known to Evelynne but unbeknownst to the Baron, Chan had stored almost every cent of what money he'd made these long years, and it would make him an older but highly eligible prize for a widow or a bride advanced in age from a fine family.

Their parting was brief. After they embraced, he took a step back and held both of her hands, as he had when she was a child. Releasing her, he bowed, and she bowed. His pale mare glistened in morning light. She pressed her hands to her chest as he mounted his horse.

"Heaven sent you," she said. Her eyes welled as her breath met the air.

Chan tipped his hat to her. "Be well, Miss Lowry."

She made the sign of the cross.

From the saddle he bowed again, solemnly.

He rode south then along the river, and she watched the line of his body in the saddle, his head tilted slightly forward over his shoulders, his hat a simple black bowler that bobbed in time to the horse. The hat moved steadily away until Chan and his horse disappeared in the trees.

She turned and drew herself into the saddle and rode north.

She had made the final break from her father.

A clean break, like severed bone.

III.

―※―

*He draws the child to his chest and lays the child
down. Outside, winter wind blows through a gap
from the Big Horns. A fire roars in the small
hearth of the stone chimney. In bed they hold the
child. He touches his wife's face. She places her
hand in his and the quiet within her is deep and
the solace within her holy.*

―※―

58.

HER FATHER WOULD pursue, she thought, and bury her hopes beneath his boot.

As she rode she told herself she would not let him find her. She'd write when she settled and promise to write him often. Even arrange to receive his letters in Billings if he so desired. In a year or so, should he agree to forgo tyranny, they could meet again. She envisioned that day, when she and Black Kettle could give him the affection he deserved.

She loved him and hated to hurt him. She hoped her father would forgive her.

WHEN THE BARON woke late the next morning, Evelynne was gone. He searched her room, then the gun cabinet. Two weapons were missing, and some clothes. He returned to her room to look out the window. He steeled his face to what he saw, the mountains and sky empty before him. He went and dressed himself precisely, black suit, black bolo tie tight to his neck. In the days to come he did the same. When he encountered people, he spoke terse, clipped words, moving like a man aware only of the steps before him. He kept much to his business and much to the chair, where he stared at the hall that led to her room.

How would he regain her? And when? His fury cloaked him like the black suits he wore. I will pursue her to the ends of the earth, he thought. I will find her, and the men with her, and crush them with my bare hands. His lips tasted sweet, his mouth was numb. Daily he raged. Nightly he passed out. An endless recursion worked at his innards.

ZION

59.

ON A NIGHT in the bleak near culminant winter Middie
emerged from a draw a short distance from camp along the path
toward the lodges. On foot, he carried a large doe like a lamb
on his shoulders. The musk of the animal lay full in his nostrils
while the cold of night surrounded him, the air, the stars, the
land robed in snow. Pale light over the plain. He saw the encampment, the lodges in a circle above the riverbed, the upper reach
of the lodge poles like hands open to the sky. The snow gave a
depth of whiteness to the world. Soon the crab apple and choke-
cherry trees would come to bloom, and the land would open
again.

He walked through a field on the approach, holding the legs
of the animal in the fist of his left hand. He carried the rifle in
his right. Thinking of Black Kettle's mother, he was reminded of
his own mother. The kindness of her eyes in the morning. He

paused, his breath a white plume from his mouth. He wanted to cry, but no tears came.

When he reached the edge of camp, he moved at a steady pace around the front of the Black Kettle lodge and saw the dark-painted buffalo above the opening, the red pulse of a fire within. He stood stock-still. A gray horse, foreleg hobbled not a length away, turned its head and eyed him, the intelligent jawline of the animal and the depth of muscle at the shoulders unmistakable.

The horse was Evelynne Lowry's.

Middie trembled. His heart became a knot of fear. He laid the doe in the snow.

As he went forward he hardly felt his feet touch the earth. He took a knee and drew the flap to a narrow crease. From the angle, hidden, he peered in. Snow gathered on his shoulders as if on granite.

Her form, outlined in black, knelt over Black Kettle. She was dressed in a long skirt and fitted coat. Her pale hands taut with vigor, she gripped William's shoulders. She leaned over him and kissed his mouth.

The motion sealed something in Middie. He stood upright and lifted his head to the sky. Zion. Only she and his mother had ever called him by that name. The stars, nestled in their cold immensity, set a course through the darkness. He left the doe, moved away from the lodge, unhobbled his own horse from a nearby stand of poplar, and passed slowly through camp. Wary of the door between this life and the next, he rode ghost-like, made vaporous by the essence of what he'd witnessed. He might pass, he thought, slim as light under the lip at the edge of the world and cross over into his mother's arms.

She waits for me, he thought.

He gave a long one-note whistle, a melody that stepped a half note down as he gathered the reins close to lift the animal's head. Though his whole body desired to cry out, he wouldn't let himself. He made a sharp click with his tongue, and the horse moved at a canter, concealed in the trees downriver from the lodges.

60.

Zion rode until dawn, his body a fortress unscaled by wind or weather. He rode until night the next day before he dismounted and crept under the dry overhang of one-hundred-foot pines along the rise of the mountains south of Billings. He snapped off tree limbs below the upper latticework of snow in the trees, taking the limbs to an open space that looked down over a wide valley, where he built a huge blaze on the mountainside. A fire tinged of red-orange tongues baleful over the plain below.

Zion was not one to hold hatred, and now his reserve broke him and tore him open and bled him out among the towns like a raw wound. Hard drink and hard fighting, he went where he went and didn't count the cost. He needed to feel the burden of blood and bone. He delivered and took beatings in the taverns he found.

Weeks later he found himself above Bozeman at the confluence of the Bridgers, the Gallatins, the Spanish Peaks, and farther south the westernmost rise of the Beartooth Range. He
built another large fire, then let it die. He sat on his heels near
the ashes for a day, a heap of snow on his back. He descended
into Bozeman like a man made of stone.

Evelynne And Black Kettle

61.

WHEN SHE ARRIVED word spread and she was taken to the Black Kettle lodge and led inside, where Black Kettle's mother touched her arm and took her to the bed of buffalo robes where Black Kettle lay. She pressed her face to his and touched his skin with her tears. She put his hands to her face and kissed them.

She looked into his eyes, held his shoulders, and kissed his mouth.

She spoke his name, but he was lost in a far country.

Astonished, Georgie and Luvinia watched Evelynne, the white woman, beautiful, the one he had told them about. She who walks from another land, they thought.

She rose and drew near.

"What has happened?" she asked.

"Raymond was killed by men in Miles City," Luvinia said.

"He grieves," Georgie said.

She watched their faces and wondered if even now her father

had begun to track her to Black Kettle, perhaps to kill him and his family. She prayed to God to protect and save. She prayed to be delivered, and for her father, she prayed for grace.

AFTER TWO MONTHS her father had not come. William received food and drink from Evelynne's hand but remained silent.

As she and Luvinia nursed William back from sorrow, Georgie approved of their concert, finding great love for Evelynne and her healing work.

Mornings Georgie took to walking with Evelynne along the Powder River. She was thin but fierce of eye. He thought she would make a good wife for his son. As they walked he motioned to the river.

"The mist rises and lies still on the water," he said.

"The sun burns it away," she said.

He thought of the years, and all the young Cheyenne men who each in their turn confronted death. The tribe clung to what remained, unsettled in this land. Their horses numbered less than three thousand now.

But Evelynne was a new creation.

"You stay because you love my son," Georgie said.

"Yes," Evelynne said.

"His heart is for you." He took her hand in his arm.

"Thank you," she said.

"Very soon he will return," Georgie said, "He no longer walks with his feet in two worlds."

"He has been gone a long time," she said. The scent of the wind was clean and leafy.

"He'll rise," said Georgie, "and his home will be your home."
Her eyes take in the world, he thought, and give back the sky.

He released her and walked toward the water. She followed and took his arm again. The river held shadows.

He put his hand in hers and stared at the water.

"Your touch heals him," he said.

"I have no one except him," she said. "I have forsaken all else."

ZION

62.

THE EARTH BENT beneath Zion, and he listened to the whistle of the train, the notes like a voice of reason in the early dark that woke and returned him, took him weary back to the loaded pull of the cars, the sound of the push and the steel of the tracks.

He'd lost his horse at Churchtree. Churchtree, bastard of a town, an eyesore of four or five wood buildings blackened at the base by mud and dust. Here men careened horses over the crest of a high ridge in a suicidal race for money, down a straight drop to the Missouri, seven horses at a time, the riders spun up good on whiskey. Few white men entered the race. The riders were mostly Cree, Assiniboine, and Sioux.

Zion shouldn't have entered, but he'd drunk himself a reservoir of liquor, and his head got the best of him. He wanted nothing really but to feel. Racing over the ridge, Zion heeled his horse full speed to the river, but halfway down he lost the horse's head and the animal's footing went all out of kilter, throwing Zion over the shoulders. Zion heard the sickening crack of the horse's neck while the other riders thundered around him and he was pummeled by the body of his horse. He lay next to the animal on the hard downslant of broken ground, his horse a length away and still as a statue. Coughing, Zion's body heaved. He felt pressure up under his rib cage and pain nearly everywhere else.

Three days' walk from Churchtree on the long expanse toward Wolf Point, he came across a wagon trail and followed in the depressed bed the tracks made. Ahead lay only plain and butte, blond grass and rock ridges.

After Evelynne and the death of his horse he carried a stone in his heart and might have nursed the loss that ate at him but for the uncommon good that met him here, far from anywhere. Midday he heard on the wind behind him the faint roll of wagon wheels. It was not long until the pinch of tack and harness came to his ear, followed by the blow of pack animals. Two pied and swayback horses pulled an empty lorry. From a distance the driver hailed him, and as Zion waved he reckoned he saw a stockman with a bushel of silver hair. But upon closer inspection the driver turned out to be an old plug-faced woman, ruddy in the cheeks, with deep-set creases around her eyes. Woolen coats thickened her chest, a brown sash wrapped her waist. She had a shotgun angled between her legs.

"Ho," she said to the horses, and they stopped on her command.

"I see you walkin'," she called down to him.

He stepped into the open grass to let her pass.

"I'll be goin' on yet," she said. Her voice was coarse.

"Yes'm," he acknowledged.

"Kind to join me?"

"Mighty good of you," he said. He set his belongings in the wagon bed and climbed up beside her. She nodded, put her nose forward like an onion bulb, and shouted, "Get up!" as she strapped the reins. The horses' buttocks flinched and the animals jumped into their traces as the wagon creaked from stall to forward motion.

"Ugly, those two," she said, pushing her lips out.

"Not pretty," he echoed.

"Get me there plenty, though," she countered. "Stubborn. Best kind. Rather walk than eat."

"Yes'm," he said. "Fine animals."

"Long about 1864 my pappy came out from Kentucky," she said. "Ten kids in tow. Mammy already dead of measle pox." Her voice had the sound of split rock. "He up and died and left us in this place." Her eyes went to the sky. "Ain't none of us ever got married, and none thought to neither.

"Only three left now," she said. "Me, my two sisters. I reckon we'll be dead soon enough."

The track was uneven. Along with the touch of their elbows and knees he was happy to hear her speak. She held the curious manner of those easy with their own voice, and she kept good humor, harrumphing on occasion as she issued a chuckle. A strain of old song from her lips from time to time, "Yo, ho, how we go! Oh, how the winds blow … white wings they never grow weary, carry me cheery over the sea … night comes, I'll stretch out my white wings and sail home to thee." Fine company, he thought. She didn't need him to speak, and he felt not a little gratitude. How comforting it was to listen.

He rode with the woman the better part of the day, saying few words, but when she paused at a simple X of wagon trails and pointed him farther north, he spoke to her directly, saying, "God sent you." She stared at him cockeyed and bellowed with laughter. Her body shook a good while.

"Never much thought of it, son," she said, wiping her eye. "People live and die."

She motioned with her jaw north. "Wolf Point is about seventy miles on."

He stepped down and pulled his gear from the wagon bed. Setting it on the ground, he removed his hat. "Kind of you, ma'am," he said.

"You lost, son?" she questioned.

"No ma'am," he said. "I don't believe so."

His face bore a pained expression.

"Keep on, son." She looked him up and down. "Find your way. Ain't a one of us ever needin' to be lost."

"Yes'm," he said.

When she clucked her tongue, the horses pushed their shoulders forward. He watched her to the horizon before he turned.

Long into the dark he laid his bedroll on open ground and slept.

THE NEXT DAY the air was cool as he went farther north among broad fields and rock outcroppings. On a long downward slope he saw movement far ahead. Growing still, he came to a crouch and sat on his heels. He broke a wand of timothy and placed it in his mouth. The cut tasted airy and dry. He pressed the stem between his teeth, feeling the tiny tube collapse as he bit at the fray. Ahead the motion he detected delighted him: a red fox more gray than red, on the hunt for mice. Four pups in the grass behind her.

He strode to a nearby knoll, where a copse of miniature birch gave shade. As he set down his bedroll and satchel he leaned his gun over them. He'd sold his saddle for almost nothing. He was glad not to carry it now. He put his back against the narrow bole of a tree and put his legs out straight.

The afternoon sun gave a white-yellow glow. There were endless undulations of land ahead of him. The fox and her pups were at play in the fields below, the pups by turns tumbling over and under each other, their yips and high-toned growls intermixed with occasional yowling. With arched back and stiff forelegs the mother pounced, nose down, flipping a mouse over her head. Zion snorted to see her eat her quarry first before catching mice for her brood. Her coat bore a hint of scarlet. The kits were grayish black, their ash-tipped tails like plumes that bounced at their backs.

He watched for a long while before the foxes went their way and he rose with the sun's descent to find a level spot to lay out his bedroll. He gathered dry grass and brush, cow chips, and a little wood and built a fire. He held his knees in his arms as the sky darkened from blue to black. A hard crescent moon hung high in the southeast. He thought of his mother and her way with God. Zion laid himself down with his chest to the fire. He had seemed cleaved in two, but today he was undivided. He rolled his boots for a pillow, crossed his arms over his chest, and slept like a dead man.

At sunrise when he brought the fire up and set bacon to butter in the cast-iron skillet the fox ascended the rise, tentative but intent. The young ones followed closely, but when they tried to move ahead she nipped at their shoulders. He drew a larger brick of bacon from the wax paper in his satchel and threw it on the skillet. The last of his store. He sat on his heels and let them come. For a moment as she topped the lip of the knoll she put her nose high and sniffed. The pups mimicked her. He took the pan from the fire, setting it on the ground. He waited. She stared. She was not the length of a man away. He drew forth a thick strip of bacon then placed it on the flat surface of a half-buried lichen-covered stone in front of him. He averted his gaze. Nose down, she crept forward. He remained still. She snatched the bacon and retreated, and the pups scattered over the lip as she gulped the bacon whole.

He took another strip, tearing it in three pieces. He set the pieces in a triangle on the stone. Again he averted his eyes. She came on with greater haste this time. Her skulk of kits followed her. She paused only for a moment, then stepped forward and took each piece delicately and ate. Only an arm's length away now she lay down with her nose on her paws. Her four kits lay beyond her. He put the pan back on the fire and let the bacon heat again.

The kits inched forward. Gray-bodied and thin, black in the forelegs, black behind the ears, they watched him with their mouths closed. He placed a strip of bacon out for each of them, and they ate ravenously.

He fed them this way until all the bacon was gone, then he

stretched out on his bedroll, watching them descend into the field until they entered a crease in the land and were gone.

He remained two days, but they did not return. He had only canned beans and salted crackers in his satchel. On the third day he slung his bedroll to his back and took up his rifle. He walked north to Wolf Point and the train.

63.

AT WOLF POINT Zion was hired by a rail foreman to work the
Empire Builder and travel to points east and west, where day was
buoyant and the night sky was a silver vestment overhead.

The older men on the line laughed at his size. They sat behind
their counters at each station and chewed their chaw. When they
spoke, they looked through him. He was nothing to them. He
let them think they owned him. He had a job, he'd bide his time.
The railroad furthered the chasm between himself and Evelynne
and the loss of all things. Something was closing over him. Often
he saw the darker image of his father's body alongside the placid
face of his mother.

Riding the Highline, he was mostly out of sight of the passengers as he hauled freight and worked coal. But a change in
duty came, one he didn't welcome. He was to provide muscle
for the boss man, the conductor, a man named Prifflach. Three

times tossing drunks to local sheriffs at the next stop, twice tracking rich old lady no-shows still wandering after the all-aboard.

Just past Bear's Paw, when the first theft among the passengers was discovered, he was put in charge of public calm. On the ride west toward the walled mountains of Glacier, he felt numb. In the first compartment the conductor leaned toward him casually in order to avoid alarm even as he yelled over the noise. First seat, worst position because of the engine's coal fire, thought Zion. He disliked Prifflach, the haughty tenor of his voice. The conductor set the course with regard to the thief. They were two towns past Bear's Paw now. "Get some leads," he said. "Happening nearly every stop. Bad for business." Then came the next town, Malta, where they found an elderly man dead, his head askew, a small well of blood in his right ear.

"He had money," said the help in the dining car. "Paid for his meals in crisp new bills. He had to have a hundred dollars or more." But when Zion checked the body, Prifflach looking over his shoulder, there was nothing, no money, not even any silver.

Prifflach's mouth tightened. "The line ain't gonna like it, guaranteed. Give me the tally."

"Four thefts now, with the dead man," Zion said in a muted voice.

"Tally his take again," said Prifflach.

Zion used a small piece of paper, a gnawed pencil. "Near four hundred dollars. Four hundred ten to be exact. Not counting what we figure for the dead man."

"Get going," Prifflach said.

Zion stared at the double doors with their elongated rectangular glass, two top squares open for the heat.

"Look alive, Middie." Prifflach slapped him on the back of the
neck.

He heard the words, noted Prifflach's face. Wet lines in a wax
head. But he stayed seated.

A weight of soot covered everyone. Passengers held children
and bags on their laps, gripping them as if to ward off death.
The train was on the upswing through great carved mountains,
and though Zion had worked the round trip from St. Paul to
Spokane a number of times already, he still felt unlanded here,
awkward under the long, slow ascent of the train and the sheer
drop of landscape from rock to trees, all the way down to the
thin, flat line of the river.

He thought of Evelynne. He pictured her walking among
the gold medallions of autumn. A stand of aspens. Her dark
wine-colored hair. Her fair face so pleasing to the eye.

The side windows remained shut. The air in the compart-
ments, especially those closest to the heat of the locomotive,
was thick to the lungs and lined with body odor. He had succeeded, through a forceful combination of the billy club Prifflach issued him and the jackknife he carried, in slightly opening the
casement adjoining his seat. Air slid through the sliver of space
even if the chug of the train tainted it all. He felt the clean blade
of pine, the rich taste of high mountains, the nicker of winter,
windy and subliminal.

Looking out, he sensed the calling an eagle might feel in the
drafts over the backbone of the continent, a feeling that some-

thing of light and stone and water, perhaps fire, had created him and breathed life through his lips. There is violence in that, he thought, as well as tenderness, and he saw as if with the eyes of a child the wings of the eagle thrown wide over the land, the scream of the bird in the high-borne wind.

64.

YET ZION'S MIND felt compressed, and he stared at everyone suspiciously.

When Prifflach rose, Zion followed. They walked a few steps and sat down again in another couplet of chairs. People were seated in a long line, from compartment to compartment, jostled by the bumps and turns of the train. They clutched their bags.

The scenario sickened him. Too many people. Too public. He'd checked the passengers three times by order of Prifflach. A full check after each of the three stops before Malta: Bear's Paw, Wolf Point, Glasgow. The first time he'd apologized, comforting an older woman on her way to see her son in Spokane. The second check more of the same, and the third, this time soothing the worry of a young woman off to the Washington state agricultural school in Pullman. Prifflach called it coincidence—three different burglars, three different towns, a little over four hundred dollars missing. Then came Malta, and the dead man. Prifflach had sent a wire at Malta inquiring what to do, and Zion had felt the minds of the people begin to hum and move. He'd sensed Prifflach, angry as if cornered, pushing him to action. Zion hated it, but the railroad had chosen him, and he was big. He'd been taught to do things right.

On that first check no one had resisted. Everyone simply wanted the thief caught. Even on the second and third checks people had remained polite, just grimacing while Zion displaced their bags and Prifflach went through them. Zion had to pat the men down, search their coats, their clothing, have them empty their pockets. It took far longer than he wished, but mostly the people smiled and tried to be helpful. But the death changed things. The women whispered and shrank away from him. The body itself, alone in a sleeping car until the next stop, was a constant reminder of the predator among them. Zion felt the tension like a vein of cloud swept into the bank of mountains, collecting, preparing.

Prifflach declared everyone must hand over their weapons and ordered Zion to gather them. The men glared as he searched their bags. Some were openly angry. Many, he thought, suspected him or Prifflach. Only a few gave up their arms, and unwillingly, a cluster of revolvers and two Derringers along with one rifle. Other men lied. Though Zion felt their weapons, in a bootleg or under the arm, he decided not to press, and Prifflach silently colluded, the potential threat quieting the conductor's zeal. What Zion retrieved he stored in the engineer's cab. Returning, he walked the aisles and felt weary.

The next stop, Havre, was a town of locked-in winters, a town of bars. At last they could remove the dead man, to be shipped back to Chicago. The body was well blanketed, taken off from the end of the train. Zion carried it across the platform, brittle and bird-like in his arms. He used his back to shield the view. Prifflach held the door for him, and as Zion entered the station he saw, over Prifflach's shoulder, the faces of passengers in the fourth car, most of them wan and dull, not wanting to meet his eye. But one, an Indian man he'd noticed on his passenger checks, looked right at him. The man had boarded the train in Bear's Paw. People had stared at him during the checks, a few uttering quiet threats while the man stared back as if taunting them to make good on their words. Even though the Indian was well dressed, Zion had had to quiet the car twice as they searched him.

Inside the station Zion heard Prifflach tell the attendant the death was of natural causes. "Old man died in his sleep," Prifflach said. "Line needs to inform the family. They can meet the body in St. Paul or wait until Chicago." Prifflach ordered Zion back to the train to watch the passengers. No sheriff, thought Zion. Railroad saving its own skin. Closemouthed, he looked at Prifflach, but the conductor waved him on, and Zion walked back to the train.

He sat in the first seat, put his head in his hands, ran his hands through his hair.

Then he disembarked, rounded the platform, and crossed the dirt street. He approached the front door of the Elk Horn Saloon. The door was painted black with oiled hinges. Inside, a dim small room and three tables, a dark marble counter with five stools. The place was clean. A lone bartender wiped things down. "Help you?" he said.

"No," Zion answered, the murmur of his voice barely audible. He needed a chair to sit in, a space to calm his mind.

The tender spat in a tin cup on the counter. "Don't drink, don't stay," he said.

Zion sensed things shutting down, his insides heavy and tight, the center of him like an eclipse that obscured the light. Three quick steps to the barman and one fist that rode the force of hip and shoulder, the man laid cold on the hardwood floor. Not dead, but still, and flat on his back. Zion, in the chair he desired, watched the blood curl from a three-inch line over the man's eye, elliptic down his face to his neck, to the floor. The tender remained motionless as Zion considered him. "Should've been Prifflach," he said aloud. But saying it made Zion feel broken. He couldn't go back. His eyes felt grave, dull as his father's. Darkness covered the earth and deep darkness its people, a darkness he could not undo. Prifflach came cursing, and Zion strode in the conductor's shadow back to the train.

As he walked the aisle, thoughts of Evelynne overcame him, the form of her, the taste of her kiss, and he knew he must do his work here now without her. He saw her stiff back and per- fectly aligned head. She walked through a field, away from him. He went to the back of the train and walked forward again as he eyed the passengers. Stuck in the clothing along his ribs, a burr needled him like a spur shank.

Three quick halts at Shelby, Cut Bank, and Browning. East Glacier next, the station at the park's east entrance with the Blackfeet Agency greeting, where three Blackfeet waited on the small wood platform in full regalia. An elder in an eagle-feath- er headdress gave out cigars. Two women in ceremonial white deerskin dresses sold beadwork. Only a handful of passengers got out and gawked. Most remained in their seats, brooding. Then, on the track past East Glacier, as the train climbed the high boundary toward the west side of the park and the depot at Belton, two more reports of impropriety, two more thefts, lesser but significant, one of fifteen dollars, the other five.

"So?" said Prifflach.

"What?" said Zion. The burr in his clothing gnawed at his side.

"So start another check," said Prifflach.

The conductor pulled a small piece of paper from his vest pocket, the wire retrieved from the Havre station in answer to his plea at Malta. Prifflach turned the paper to Zion and read the words: *Keep quiet—no police—security man finds thief—or loses job.*

"No good," said Zion aloud, using a tone he'd heard his mother use to calm his father. "Look at them," Zion said, motioning with his eyes down the aisle.

Prifflach turned on him, sharp-faced, and what he said made Zion desire to kill him. "Line's takin' you out if you don't get it done, boy. Now, move!"

Zion saw it coming, and he wished against it, but he knew no alternative. Heavy-shouldered, he rose from his seat. He began again.

"Pardon me, can I see your bag?" The words sounded rough in his mind, his body too warm and lathered like a horse.

65.

PEOPLE BECAME OPENLY hostile now. A woman in the first car and one in the third made a scene and wouldn't unhand their bags. He pulled the bags from the two and let Prifflach search the contents. When he approached a third woman, she clawed a hole in his cheek.

He recoiled and stared at her.

Her face was a mountain of red.

Some of the other passengers helped him with the woman, holding her for him. What am I doing? Zion thought. They see it too. They all understand this doesn't make sense. Still Prifflach gave the bag a thorough inspection. When Zion returned it to the woman, she railed at him. "God curse you," she said and turned her back.

He walked from the third car toward the fourth, opening and closing the double doors at the end of the compartment. He stood on the deck, heard the raw howl of the train, the wind. Something will happen now, he thought.

To his left a wall of wet granite rolled, hard and black, blurred by the train speed. The rock face reached upward thousands of feet, jagged and pinnacled at the top as it swept out over the train. Beyond this the gray sky was low and thick. It gave him vertigo, and he turned his head down and gripped the handrail. Seeing his worn boots on the grated steel, he couldn't remember his mother's face.

To his right the valley spread wide in a pattern of darks and lighter darks, filled from above by the distant pull of fog and heavy rain. The downpour fell in wide diagonal sheets, descending into massive rock shelves far on the other side of the valley. Among the bases of the mountains, forests robed the land like cloaks. The water ran hard from the runoff of the storm, and everything converged to a river turned coal black.

The river was the middle fork of the Flathead, past the summit of Marias Pass and past the great trestle of Two Medicine Bridge. They had crested the Great Divide. The train's muscle pumped faster now, louder on the westward downgrade. The river ran due west from here, seeming to bury itself into the wide, forested skirt of a solitary land mass. The flat-topped tower of the mass was mostly covered by wet fog but visible in its singularity and the ominous feel of something hidden in darkness, something entirely individual, accountable to neither sky nor storm. The hulk of the land felt gargantuan. He couldn't make out if it was Grinnell Point or Reynolds Mountain, Cleveland or Apikuni. Montana, he thought dimly, land of one hundred mountain ranges.

Here in his reverie, muffled shouts came faint like the far-off cry of a cat. He looked up to the doors of the final passenger car. Slender windows framed his view and suddenly the disembodied words came to him: "I've got him! I've got the mother-hatin' rat."

Zion leapt forward, opening the fourth car, shouting, "Stop! Wait!"

About midway up the car a heavyset man along with four others had thrown someone to the floor in the aisle. The man wore a brown tweed suit and struggled vigorously with his assailants.

"It's him!" cried the heavier one. "We caught him red-handed."

The other passengers pressed back against the walls. Women pushed their wide-eyed children behind them.

"Let go," said Zion, staring at the fat man. The men heeded his word quickly and without complaint. People harbor fear, he thought, and he recognized the sway he held, over people, over men. They viewed him as rock or landslide, not man.

The captive stood in the aisle and brushed wrinkles from his suit, his hair flung forward, black and thick over his face. Dark-eyed. The Indian.

When the man pushed his hair back, the bones of his face appeared chiseled in stone. His body was angular, the skin thin as a sheet of newsprint, ready to tear open, Zion thought, ready for it all to break out. But the man tucked in his shirt and realigned his belt. He straightened his vest, then the lapels of his jacket, visibly pulling the tension in and down, breathing. He was silent. He viewed his captors, each one, with contempt.

Zion pictured his firm step and upright gait when the man had first walked the aisle and positioned his bags. Assiniboine or Sioux, he'd thought. But after pulling his bag and questioning him he'd found him to be a Blackfeet-white cross, a Blood in fact—a Blackfeet subtribe—and Irish on the other side. He was on his way to his family's home south of West Glacier after a trip to Bear's Paw. The man said he taught at the college in Missoula. In education, he said. They had locked eyes when Zion had carried the dead man at Havre, but Zion had dismissed it, and other than the agitation of the crowd during the checks, an agitation that seemed always to accompany Indians and whites, he'd found nothing unusual. The Indian carried no weapon.

"What is it?" Zion asked the heavy one.

A short man with slick hair, one of the others who'd held the accused, spoke up. "This man"—he pointed in the Indian's face— "this man's been lying! He's the one. He took all the money."

"Slow down," said Zion. "Say what you know."

"I have not lied," said the prisoner.

"Shut up!" the slick-haired man yelled.

Zion put a forearm to the slick one's chest. "Settle yourself," he said.

The man sat down but whispered and glared. "He's lying," he said. "Hiding something."

"How do you know?"

"Check his side, see for yourself. He's had his hand in his jacket from the start."

The heavy man butted in, edging with rage. "He won't show us what he's got in there." His head was large and flushed.

"Is it true, sir?" asked Zion, working to be polite. "Is there something hidden in your vestcoat?"

"Yes," he stated, looking into Zion's face, "but that doesn't make me a liar and doesn't make me guilty either."

"We will check it, sir," Zion replied, but he was angry. The taste of metal came to his mouth. He didn't like the tone the Indian had used. "What have you concealed?" Zion asked.

"My money belt," said the man.

Zion hardened his look. His hands began to sweat. He wiped them on his pant legs as he stared at the Blackfeet man. The money belt had been there the whole time, probably thin as birch bark on his waistline, concealed under the clothing. He remembered Prifflach muttering under his breath at the Indian as he checked the man's bag, a small cylindrical briefcase made of beaten brown leather, sealed at the top by a thin zipper that ran between two worn handles, the word MONTANA inscribed on the side.

"You've searched my briefcase and my wallet," said the man, "and me once more than the others. I saw no need for you to search my money belt. And if I had shown you, don't you think it would have become a target for the robber if he were in this compartment during the search?"

"Don't listen to him," the slick one said. "He's slippery."

The crowd murmured uneasily. Outside, the fog had pressed in. Nothing of the valley could be seen, and nothing of the sky. *The mountains will be laid low*, Zion thought. The words came to him, soft and articulate in his mother's voice. He saw the featureless gray of a massive fog bank and behind it a feeling of the bulk of the land.

"Check his belt," the fat one said.

Then the crowd began. "See what he's got," said a red-haired woman, the fat man's wife by the look of it. She said the words quietly, but they were enough to hasten a flood. "Do it now," heard Zion. "Make him hand it over"; "Take it from him"; "Pull up his shirt"; "Take it"—all from the onlookers, all at once, and from somewhere low and back behind Zion the words "Cut his throat."

The conductor, arrived and Zion exhaled, feeling his body go slack. Zion stared outside. The storm leaked moisture on the windows. The moisture gathered and drew the lines sideways, rivulets like tiny rivers pulled along the glass to the end of the train.

Evelynne And Black Kettle

66.

As luvinia kneeled over William she took an eagle fan from her pouch and waved it over him, singing to him in the presence of Evelynne. The rich smell of fetid earth rode the wind along with the acrid scent of stinkweed. Inside the lodge, deer and grouse and sage hen bubbled in a pot over the fire, mixing with the airy taste of pine.

Luvinia waved the fan over his chest and up over his face and eyes. She sang her healing song, her song for the new day. It was the song of Sweet Medicine, and it moved from her lips like wind, the song from Luvinia Black Kettle to William from before he was born.

In the song, Sweet Medicine entered the lodge with the sacred arrow bundle and said, "People of the Tsitsistas, with a great power I am approaching. Be joyful. I bring the sacred arrows. You have not yet learned the right way to live. That is why the Ones above were angry and the buffalo went into hiding." Sweet

Medicine filled a deer-bone pipe with sacred tobacco. Night came, and by firelight he taught the People what the spirits inside the holy mountain had taught him.

And these teachings became the way of the Tsitsistas, a good way.

67.

AT THE ADVENT of dawn on a day in late autumn with the trees colored in the lowlands and the sun strong in the sky, Evelynne sat near William and placed her hand on his head. She touched his face. Her body so near astonished him.

He noted the base of the lodge, the line of darkness along the foot of the lodge poles where the hide had been stretched taut and the sun sought entry and appeared to burn a broken line in a circle on the ground around them. The poles went up through the smoke hole. He placed a hand on the lodge pole nearest him and followed it upward, marveling at the closeness and release a man received in the presence of a woman.

"How do you feel?" he asked her.

"Beautiful," she answered as he drew her to his chest.

The bones of her cheek were pressed to the rise of his body, and she envisioned the membrane of touch that separated them as if it were nothing until finally she could see herself completely inside him. She had never once been this close to a man. She closed her eyes, listening to the sound of William's heart as it beat in his chest like a slow, deep drum.

A little while later he rose, robed himself in buffalo hide, and walked the land, his figure like a day ghost among the trees along the river, his hair mane-like behind him. She and his mother and father followed. When he reached the water, he removed the buffalo robe and stepped naked into the flow. When he emerged, the cold light of morning was on him. His skin shone, and his mother wrapped him in a long blanket as his father sang a victory song.

Overhead was the white-blue pan of day.

ZION

68.

"MAKE HIM HAND over that money belt directly," said Prifflach, his face pinched and set like clay. Pressure built in the body cage of Zion. He gripped the accused man's wrist, latching on to the flesh with frozen fingers, and did not let go.

To Zion's relief, the man submitted. With one arm in Zion's grip, the man used his free hand to untuck the front of his shirt. He slid the money belt to a point above his waist as he undid the small metal clasps that held the belt in place. His fingers are meticulous, thought Zion, his eyes as clear as the sky before they reached Glacier but cold and steely-black. Zion looked again to the window. His own reflection was not unlike the gray outside. Behind it lay the unpeopled weight of land, the emptiness. Zion's fists felt big and hard. He thought of his mother. He saw her again, smiling as she came forth and called to him from afar. Zion, she said, *do not fear me, but receive me.*

"Give up the belt," Prifflach said, though already the man was pulling it free.

He held it out to the conductor. "Nothing out of the ordinary," he said. "I'm simply a man carrying my own money."

At once the heavyset man and his wife shouted something unintelligible.

"We'll see," said the conductor, interpreting their words. "We'll see if it's his money." At the corners of Prifflach's mouth the skin twitched. Prifflach took the money belt and handed it to the slick man. "Count it up," he said, watching the Indian's face.

The slick man thumbed the money once, finding a combination of bigger and smaller bills.

"How much is there?" asked the conductor. The slick man counted again, slowly.

"Five hundred thirty dollars," he said.

Zion knew a desire gripped them. They all calculated the old dead man's loss at a clean one hundred.

"I could have told you that," said the accused.

"Shut up," Prifflach said, then added, "a hundred dollars more than the total." He folded the money belt in half, and half again. "I'll take that," he said, placing it in the chest pocket of his coat.

It came clear to Zion now, from the look of the other passengers, they'd all torn loose inside, all come unspun. He remembered what he'd read in a pamphlet at the West Glacier station a month ago. Something about a hidden passage west, close to the headwaters of the Marias, a high mountain pass that according to Blackfeet belief was steeped in the spirit world, occupied by a dark presence. Decades back, when the line first wanted to chart its track through here, no Indian would take a white man through. Death inhabited the place.

The demeanor of the Blackfeet man changed. The man's face lost expression, his body pulled inward. In the space between them Zion sensed the man gather himself. Zion tightened his grip. The crowd moved.

"Suspected him back in Glasgow," one man piped up. "I should have known," said another. And from the slick man, "He ain't gettin' outta here." In a graveled tone, deep back in the crowd again, a voice said, "Slit his throat."

The movement began in words and rustling, then leapt up like a mighty wind that broke upon the people and the Blackfeet man all at once. The man jerked free and jumped the chair back next to him, seeking to flank them and escape from the rear of the compartment. The men scrambled after him, Prifflach leading as the others followed, all of them livid with anger turning to hate.

Zion vaulted a set of chairs and landed on the Blackfeet man, slamming him against the sidewall of the car. The man righted himself and spat in Zion's face, and Zion lifted him, encircling the man's head in both his hands. He propped him up, putting his left hand on the man's shoulder, and leveled a blow with the right that bounced the Blackfeet man's head off the near window and flung his hair like a horsetail. The man gritted his teeth and spat at Zion again as four other men surrounded him, dragging him back toward the rear of the car. As the Indian lurched forward, his head snapped back on his neck.

"What are you doing?" he cried out. Straining at the hands that grasped his upper body, he turned his face to the window, to the gray valley beyond, and said, "I have a wife. I have a child."

With shocking swiftness the man threw his forearms out and lunged forward with his head in order to strike someone. But his flailings were as nothing to the weight of his accusers. They were a mob now. They punched him in the back and in the back of the head. "Thief!" they said. "Murderer." The group was packed in, forming a tight, untidy ball in the aisle and among the spaces between the seats. A thick odor met the air.

The prisoner's head was near the floor. Reaching for the Blackfeet man's waist, Zion saw a look of resignation, a look of light among the features of his face. The man stared at Zion and whispered something he could not hear or understand.

Amid the tumult a smaller voice called out, "Wait!" It came from behind Zion, up near the far end of the car. Looking back through the moving heads, back behind the bending, pressing torsos, Zion saw a small man, adolescent in appearance, thin-boned in a simple two-piece suit. He had fine blond hair and oval wire-rimmed glasses.

"Wait!" the man said. "I know him."

A large man at the back of the mob turned to him and said, "Shut your mouth."

The small man's face went red. He shrank back to his seat. Zion turned to the mob. The people grabbed at the Blackfeet man's clothing and shook his body like a rag doll. The man's limbs appeared loose, the arms moving as if boneless, as if the elbows were disconnected from the shoulders.

Zion saw the little man with his head down now as the commotion swirled toward the head of the car, down to the doors they had already pulled back and the opening to the platform tilted like a black mouth from which the wind screamed. Zion heard the accused grunting, cursing. The little man rose and walked directly to the rearguard of the mob. Unable to get through, he sidestepped the knot of people. Repositioning women and children, he climbed over three or four seats, awkwardly like a leggy insect, toward the front of the compartment and the landing beyond. The prisoner was being held about the neck by the thick hands of Prifflach, still clenched about the waist by Zion and on both sides by angry men. Prifflach, with blood-red face and lips pulled near to his ears, pressed the wedge of his nose against the Indian's head.

The small man mounted the arms of the last two aisle chairs so that he stood directly before the mob. He straddled the aisle, the open doorway behind him, the land outside a blur and around him the live wind a strange unholy combustion. He drew his fists to his sides, billowed his chest as he gathered air, and screamed, "Stop!" A scream high and sharp like the bark of a dog.

69.

THE LITTLE MAN'S effort created a brief moment of quiet. The conductor held firm but turned a white eye to him. Seizing this, the little man strung his words rapidly. "I know him. I spoke with him when he got on in Bear's Paw. He has a three-year-old daughter. He has a wife. He has a good mother, a good father. He will be dropped off at the stop on the far side of Glacier, where they are waiting for him. He will return with them by automobile to the Mission Range."

"Shut up," said Prifflach.

"I won't," said the small man. "He told me precisely."

"He lied," said the slick man.

"Let me speak," the small man pleaded. He touched his hand to his temple, a gesture both elegant and tremulous.

"We won't," the mob responded, and in the pronounced gather of their voices and by their movement the prisoner was lifted by the neck and shoved forward toward the door. The mob smelled of heat and urgency.

"Out of the way!" the fat man yelled, and Zion watched as the small man took a blow to the side of his head, a shot that lifted him light as goose down, unburdened in flight to where his body hit the wall near the floor of the car. "Before all of this, he had five hundred thirty dollars." Zion's fists were bound up in the clothing of the Blackfeet man, his forearms bone to bone with the man's ribs. The little man continued. "He meant to do what he and his wife dreamed. He meant to buy land, off the reservation." The voice seemed small, down between the chairs, "He meant to build a house. A home."

A weight of bodies pressed Zion from behind, but he needed his hands to control the captive. The opening through which they were pushed was wide, the landing now beneath their feet solid and whole, like a long-awaited rest. Zion could hear the velocity of wind and steel as he flowed with the crowd to the brink.

He wanted to cry or cry out. He felt the imprint of the guardrail firmly on his thigh and saw the chasm between this car and the next. He heard the small man's voice back behind him. "He told me at Bear's Paw—precisely five hundred thirty dollars. Five hundred thirty."

70.

THE LANDING WAS narrow, the people many, and they were
pushed by a score or more men running from other cars, clog-
ging the aisle to get to the man. Those at the front gripped the
railing and grappled with each other. Noise surrounded them,
the train's cry, the wide burn of descent, the people's yells high
above everything, shrill as if from the mouths of predatory birds.
The Blackfeet man's suit coat and vest were gone. His slim upper
body looked clean in his worried shirt, his V-shaped torso trim
and strong.

In the press of it Zion was hot. Ox-like, he sensed the burden of everyone, borne at once in him. He wanted to hold the
Blackfeet man fast, but instead the crowd shoved the man aloft.
They tipped him upside down and clutched his ankles as they
removed his shoes. They tore off his shirt, then his ribbed un-
dershirt. They threw the shoes down among the tracks. Prifflach
shouted obscenities. The clothing was thrown out into the wind,

where it whisked away, rolling and descending like white leaves down into the fog of the valley.

Somehow the man was lowered between the cars. Below him Zion saw the silvery gleam of the tracks, parallel lines in the black blur of the ties, the lines bending almost imperceptibly at times, glinting dull like teeth. With his elbows he tried to hold the mob back. The Blackfeet man closed his eyes and moved his lips. He gripped Zion's forearms, and Zion stared into his face. The man spoke in a strange tongue. Zion felt the oncoming force of the crowd behind him. A woman's voice rose, a voice he knew but did not recognize. He bowed his back and groaned, trying to draw the man forth. The words were repeated like a song, simple and beautiful in his mind: *Put on your garments of splendor.* He smelled the oil of the train, the heat, the wet rock of the mountain.

He set his jaw and strained. He would pull the people and the man and the entire world to the mercy of his will.

He gained no ground.

The speed of the train and the noise of the tracks, the scent of high sage and jack pine, the fogged void of gray as wide and deep as an ocean. But foremost the wind rushed up against the mob, creating an almost still-life movement into which they carried the man. Then the wind died. The river of people flowing from the compartment bottlenecked in the doorway. Zion said, "No! This must stop!" He gripped the Blackfeet man's belt with both fists and pulled him upward. As he strained to draw the man forth, his big body was a countermovement against the rise of all around him, but the mob grew to an impossible mass that pushed and swelled and in a sudden gush broke free. Zion found himself with the Blackfeet man airborne, cast into the gulf without foot or handhold. He had lost everything, and, falling, he saw a shaft of blue high in the gray above him and was surprised at how light he felt and how time had slowed to nothing. He reached back, seeking a purchase he would not find, but in the singular sweep of his arm he took people unaware—Prifflach, the fat man, his wife, the slick man—they too flew from the edge, effortless in the push of the mob, unstrung bodies and tight faces, over the lip of the guardrail and down between the cars, down to the tracks, the wheels, the black pump of the smoking engine, the yell of the machine.

Evelynne And Black Kettle

71.

When black kettle returned to the lodge, he watched his father draw the flaps back from the opening. His mother and Evelynne had gone ahead, and now his mother sat before the fire, her strong back to him as she combed Evelynne's hair with her fingers. William came near, kneeling to sit with them. His mother began to set Evelynne's hair in thick braids.

Evelynne liked the feel of Luvinia's fingers as they smoothed and parted and drew her hair fast. Evelynne had waited all her life. Her patience rested now in the hope of a family to whom she gave herself without reservation and from whom she would receive a man who would be closer to her than a brother. As Luvinia braided Evelynne's hair, the quiet that fell in the lodge was a gift.

She thought of the years with her father and the tyrant in him. She had passed through fire to arrive here on the threshold of her wedding to William. Of William her mother might approve from her place in heaven, but her father would demand a reckoning. Would he come to Tongue River country? She begged God that he would not. She asked God to hold her father fast. Quiet his spirit, she prayed.

As William sat down at an angle beside her and let his back rest against hers, she felt the warmth of his body. She pressed into him, and he absorbed her weight. She smiled. The soul of man is a house of hope, she thought. A home. But life would not be easy here. She reached and held William's wrist.

AMONG THE STRANGE new events she encountered, Evelynne danced her first round dance. She had rarely felt so awkward. So beheld by curious eyes. A drum like the feet of giants on the mountain, the men singing loud and high, like coyotes, she felt removed from her own body as she walked in a large circle with the others. They were cloaked in clothing contemporary or traditional, the men in cowboy hats of varied heights and shapes or hatless, their hair braided and tied in blue and red cloth or hair straight and long, set with down-facing feathers. The women draped themselves in shawls and woolen blankets. They wore dresses decorated with elk teeth, porcupine quills, and bead patterns. The men wore shirts from which ribbons tailed like strands of colored smoke.

For Evelynne, the night would have remained awkward but for William's father, Georgie, who came and danced beside her, teaching her the simple two-step beat. He took her arm in his, helping her, even in all her uncommon apparel: her tight burgundy waistcoat lapeled and tailored under a fitted jacket, a fluted skirt that flared near the ground, black cowboy boots custom-made by the best boot makers west of the Mississippi. She wore wine-red gloves and silver hair combs that held her hair up in a decadent tower. Georgie nearly pranced her through the rhythms before they began to settle over her while she went with him at a steady pace.

Still she felt untoward. She glanced over her shoulder. William watched her.

Georgie stayed close, motioning for her to unloose herself. She tried to open her frame and make her arms sway, but her gait was wooden. Finally he undid his braid ties, unwinding each braid in order to let down his hair. He shook his head, and his hair flowed behind him. The drum boomed like a great heart. The cry of the singers soared. He gestured to her, and the entire circle looked upon her. William's mother Luvinia drew near, and Raymond's mother came alongside, pressing her shoulder gently to Evelynne's shoulder as she held her hand. Evelynne's neck and face reddened. She was unsure of herself, but she grew quiet and, listening, ascertained the right path. She took off her gloves. She gathered Raymond's mother's hands in hers and gave the gloves to her, and Raymond's mother wore them, waving to the tribe, her face beaming as everyone grinned. Then Evelynne removed her combs, letting her hair fall full to her waist. She approached Luvinia and placed the combs in her hair. Evelynne thought Luvinia looked stunning as the combs shone in the light of fires. Luvinia's face shimmered in the darkness. The people whistled to Evelynne, and she blushed again. But as William danced beside her, the rigidness left her and she was at peace.

EQUALLY STRANGE TO her, Eve's next experience was touched
by grit and bone. Luvinia brought her to a group of women
who prepared animal hides a short distance from the wooden
frames where raw strips of elk meat hung to dry. The women sat
on the ground, and Luvinia and Evelynne sat down with them.
Evelynne was given a dark stone that fit smoothly in the palm
of the hand. The upper edge was sharp as a blade. Evelynne's
thumb fit an indentation on the surface. The stone had good
weight.

Luvinia directed Evelynne's hand to the hide, and the wom-
en murmured, then chuckled at seeing Evelynne work among
them. "They laugh at you," Luvinia said, motioning with her
hand to her eyes. "They see you." Evelynne nodded, setting to
work, but she did not look up. Together they removed hair and
blood with the thumb scrapers until the surface was clean. Then
they stretched the hide and set it to dry upon the wooden rack.
When it had hardened and dried, the women would piece it out,
chewing the leather for moccasins, gloves, and purses. The day's
hunt had been good. They cleaned three more hides, and by the
time they were done her fingers bore the stain of blood. Her nail
beds were slick with animal fat.

William noticed from a distance and came near, his own hands
dyed darker than hers. Skinning the elk, he and the other men
had pulled out the entrails, backstrapped and quartered the animals, and cut off the hoofs. They'd harvested all the edible parts
for cooking or drying. His arms were coated almost to the shoulders in blood. He touched her forearm, so she rose to follow
him, down toward the river through head-high willows to the

water's edge. Walking, they flushed a mountain bluebird and watched it glide low over the water, the sky-blue flare of wings opening to white as it flew to the arm of a cottonwood on the other side. They stepped into the water together, coming to a still point in the flow near the cut edge of a shoal. A rush of cold met her legs. Her dress bloomed at her waist before it darkened and began to mix and move in the water. William stood with her as they washed the blood away. For all his faults, her father had given her strength. She could survive here, she thought, even thrive. Evelynne looked on William with deep regard. His smile was wide and full. She could not have imagined for herself a life more odd, nor one more complete.

EVELYNNE DESIRED TWO ceremonies, and so it was they were married once on a cut bank above the Powder River, where she wore a cloth wool dress inlaid with elk bone and ivory eyeteeth while he wore the regalia of a soldier chief, deerskin and fringe patterns and eagle feathers. Evelynne was named White Woman Standing for how she had stood upright since she'd come to the Cheyenne, her back straight as a lodge pole, her thin arms like reeds at her sides.

The second ceremony was of equal import to her and the Black Kettle clan.

In accord with the Catholic sisters at the school outside Lame Deer, Evelynne Lowry in white lace dress with hat and veil was promised to William Black Kettle in black suit, white shirt, black vest, and bolo tie with a turquoise stone. The crisp scent of his tailored suit was a comfort to her. When she and William emerged from the one-room schoolhouse, she shouted and the people laughed, drawing near in order to touch her hair and hat and dress.

After a meal of venison and wild turnips prepared by the sisters, Evelynne and William rode their horses on a tandem canter to where the land lifted and the sky circumscribed a span as blue as a robin's egg. They slowed, letting the horses walk a sandstone rim as she and William spoke sweetly to one another.

HER POETRY CONTINUED without abeyance, taking on more conjugal motifs. Purpose and cross-purpose, the chrysalis and the butterfly, violence, touch and forgiveness, night and home. She wrote most during winter, when the heat of the fire was up and days fell toward nights in which she and William spoke to one another, taking their journey to where she found in him a true generosity. They created from no knowledge a knowledge no other shared and that became to them cherished. Their knowledge was infused with stories of childhood, growing up, and family, through the crushing blows one experienced with age. William read her poems out loud at day's end, and she gave herself over to the rapture of his countenance.

"My father read my poems aloud," she said.

"Your father is with you," William responded.

She noticed an undefined but definite order to the tribe, to men and women and children, and a black sorrow that could not be fully named. At night, the stars. In the morning, dawn. There was ferocity and laughter. Dance and quiet. Who was she among them? She felt like a ghost, pale but physical. She missed her father, but her place was here, where they loved her beyond curiosity and without need. In William's arms she no longer desired to fly away. She could wholly love this earth.

On occasion William would ride with her to Lame Deer where she sent forth poems and received return word of her poetry alive in the world: publications in London, Amsterdam, and Paris; continued recognition in the *Atlantic Monthly*; even a dignified invitation from the princess of Siam to read in the courts of the king. In all this Evelynne never failed to write her father.

But from his hand no word came.

The Baron

72.

A YEAR PASSED, two. More.

The Baron fell into an oblivion in which he hardly rose from his bed.

She was gone. She stayed gone.

He knew she would not come back.

The air he breathed, laboring, seemed to crumble like dirt into the edge of his mouth, and he had a hard time expelling it. His chest hitched upward. He took short breaths. He hacked to clear his lungs.

He believed he would die soon. He felt doom. The doctors came and took his money, telling him he might live a long time yet, but he saw the deceit in their eyes.

His thoughts went forth like white birds into the life he had lived and returned dark-winged and black of beak.

He'd killed three men in his lifetime.

The second was accidental, during the early years on the ranch when a Chinese stable boy named Liu spooked Josef's horse and Josef was thrown. Enraged, he rose, lifted his pistol, and struck Liu behind the head. Liu fell forward like a boulder, hit the ground face first and didn't move. Nothing for it, Josef, thought then. A man lives and dies.

The third death occurred in a drunken brawl in Virginia City when he was nearly fifty. Just off the boardwalk in the street outside the saloon, a larger man kicked Josef in the back. Josef threw him to the ground before he grabbed the man's head and shoved cold dirt into the mouth and eyes. He straddled the man's chest, cuffing his skull and beating his cheek in front of the ear. But it was only when he punched the man's throat and felt the windpipe collapse that he saw the eyes go out. Night's darkness. Fights as common as drink in that town, he walked back into the saloon, gambled till dawn, and fell asleep in his chair with his head on the table. Even the tender went to bed before first light. Josef never told his daughter, and he was glad he had not.

He didn't lament either of those two deaths. The first killing, though, still bothered him and could not be dislodged. Before Montana, before all this, in a rage he'd killed his own brother.

He remembered now how his wife loved his brother like her own, and how it was a hard task to earn her forgiveness, though they both knew the largest portion of the fault lay not with him but with his brother. The memory always near the surface, Josef's stomach still rose when he thought of his drunken father and brother plotting against him after his first big windfall in St. Louis. He would have shared the money with them, but he needed it to stepladder to bigger ventures.

Brother Leopold took more after their father, pink-skinned, often jovial, large and round with brown-gold hair that shone like stalks of mown wheat. And Josef himself was more of mother than father, willful, slender, and brooding, with black hair and pale white skin. A man of commerce, commanding and shrewd, he would do his father proud or so he thought. Leo was obtuse and self-serving yet doted on by their father. A nature so unseemly, Josef didn't understand how his father could be so smitten.

NEAR A STOCKYARD along the river at night, the two fought, with their father looking on, to be rid of one another. The night was filled with rain and the ground slick, but Leo advanced quickly, cutting Josef's chest in a fast arc shoulder to shoulder. A violent surge came to Josef then, and he rushed Leo, grappling upward as he held his brother's forearms, jerking his hands swiftly to dislodge the knife. Handle up, the blade fell, and they both went to the ground but Josef reached it first, rolling as he stuck the blade three times into Leo's side.

Lying at a slant, Leo groaned as Josef stood over him and watched him die.

That night Josef and his wife passed on horseback through a bowl of low mountains, where they heard a slight cry of wind over the fields and far off the sound of crickets, the call of birds. The wind carried the musky scent of bear. He breathed it in, aware of a danger robust enough to change a man's fortune. The sunflowers that tipped their heads along the path, tall as the shoulder of his horse, wafted dust and tinder, an unpleasant weedy scent that brought water to his eyes. Above this the pines smelled faintly of winter. To the south the silver sheen of a large lake seemed to anoint the night with clarity.

Josef prayed then with his wife listening. In the starlight he rode with her among a vastness of trees, earth, and sky, flower, insect, and animal. He settled into a gait to carry them long and well, and far away.

Now, in his bed, remembering, he touched the silk border of the coverlet. His breathing had gone wheezy.

He would be dead soon. He could no longer convince himself otherwise. His wife and son were lost to him. His daughter, Eve. In the evening light of the house in Butte he wished now he had loved his brother more. His mother and father. All of them. Or at least had the chance to love them again. But what was done was done and could not ever be undone. The days had taken him west, where he'd built his empire. Here he had thought to secure his legacy—first through his son, Tomás, second through Evelynne. Hadn't he given them the best of all things? Not just shelter and clothing but wealth, the finest education, opportunity, society? There was a sudden piercing in his chest.

He wished, after everything, they could be with him now. His son, Tomás. Eve in her loveliness and grace.

He fell asleep and did not wake.

73.

NOT THREE YEARS from the day his daughter left him, Josef Lowry was dead.

To those who knew him best in business, he'd been obtuse and self-aggrandizing, ruthless in his hunger for empire. The collapsed heart that performed his demise was the same he had hidden from men and given as fully as he knew how to his wife.

WHEN EVELYNNE LEARNED of his passing, she set out with William for Butte. Nights, they camped under open skies. When they were a day's ride out, William drew his horse onto a great plain. She rode beside him and heard the cry of a hawk like a torn page in the stillness. William had been to her what she had not thought possible, a kind of freedom.

She let William's horse go before hers over the plain that had seemed in the morning uncrossable but by day's end had become a journey they set behind them. What would the funeral be? The viewing of her father. Dread filled her. She imagined ravenous townsfolk with feral eyes. She rode with her head down, her hands crossed over the pommel.

The bleed of sun diminished and died away.

74.

Dawn found her with William back in the place where she'd spent the years of her life before their marriage.

People stared. Not a few spit on the ground. Some turned away.

They went first to the mansion in the city. The house was empty. On her father's desk in the front room she found a copper box with all her letters.

She went to her bedroom and gathered her funeral clothes.

At the private viewing, she wore appropriate attire for the daughter of a baron, the same she'd worn in mourning her brother. Her face was hidden. When she removed her gloves, her hands looked like white birds.

She clutched the bundle of letters in her left arm. Her father's casket was twice as big as any she'd seen, made entirely of copper. The insides were covered with pillowed white cloth. Lifting her veil, she leaned her upper body over the lip and looked in. He was worse for wear than she had hoped. His hair stood powdered and stiff, the hands and face tinted orange. It wasn't him. The copper lit his skin. She saw the marks she'd made on his face as a young woman.

His voice had taught her reverence for both word and wilderness. She had left him because she needed to, and yet she remembered his tenderness to her. The image of his palm cupped to her cheek when she was a girl came to her, and she folded inward and placed her arms on his chest and convulsed as she wept. Beneath all his ambition he'd been only a man, she thought.

Over commerce and copper he'd acquired mastery, a man whose command gained mountains and millions. The coffin itself, beveled and multifaceted, high-walled with a domed lid, glowed like the sun and attested to his stillborn hopes, a sarcophagus like an ill womb.

She placed her hands firmly on his arm, leaned over him and kissed his forehead. His hands were straight to his sides. The twill of his coat was abrasive. Her tears fell on his shirt. The body was unsightly with his stiff white collar starched and pressed, his copper cufflinks inlaid like nails in the buttonholes at his wrists. She stared at the coffin lid, open like a door that led down into the ground.

FROM THE BACK of the church William beheld Evelynne. Her face was a lantern in the black of her accoutrements. The dead man, her father, below her, William thought, remained unsatiated. To where does his spirit flee?

SHE PLACED HER letters between her father's forearm and the side of his body. Drawing her mother's crucifix from her vest pocket, she placed it on his chest, and lifted her eyes. She laid her head on his shoulder, saying, "Forgive me Father." She kissed his forehead again, making the sign of the cross before she drew her veil over her face, rose, and went with William, out into the sunlight.

75.

THE FUNERAL PROCESSION was a belt of opulence in the gray of the city. On the path to the graveyard, the road wound its way, and from the dark openings of alleys people jostled one another as they gasped at the transparent tower that stood atop a lorry pulled by fourteen black horses. The coffin, encased by four panes of glass, was nearly unbearable to the eye. Two suns, she thought, the sun in the sky and the sun of the coffin.

People shaded their eyes with a fan or a felt hat, but Evelynne stared straight ahead, her horse in stride with William's a few paces behind the funeral carriage. Her tears fell hot on her cheeks. Her brother first and now her father.

Tomorrow the papers would headline the spectacle of the funeral alongside the spectacle of her with Black Kettle, subservience and loathing in their tone.

The road took a sharp turn uphill away from the buildings into open ground until it banked through the granite entry to Mount

Moriah Cemetery. When the horses stopped, she stood over the burial site with William, the earth open like a mouth for her father's body.

The sun had fallen, and shadow cloaked the mountain. She had heard he wanted to be buried in copper and the copper then buried in the mountain, returned like a mother lode, she thought, distorted and beautified. William was beside her as the men lowered the casket by rope and pulley into the ground. A thousand years would pass before the metal regained itself and the dust of his bones rejoined the earth. Within a month's time a house of Rhode Island granite, pillared and set with fleur-de-lis, apexed by a thick square cross, would stand over the grave. In elegant cursive *The Baron Josef Lowry* would be carved above a white marble door.

In the dark of the hole the coffin glimmered. She felt William's arms around her. She held no contempt for her father. His pride had harmed him. He was a creature of harm. People suffered his cruelty. Dead, his hand was stayed.

EVELYNNE

76.

AFTER THE FUNERAL she went to the ranch house and entered the front doors into the great room, where the predators
gathered to lay claim to her father's empire. Men with eyes like
funnels in the skull. She walked among them, and they let her
pass. Box and satchel in hand, William accompanied her. As he
set his look on the men, she noted his eyes were fierce. Turning
from them, they ascended the great stair to the bedroom.

She closed the door behind William, setting the box he'd
brought from the city house on the bed. She unlaced her dress,
folded it neatly and positioned it inside. He placed the satchel on
the floor beside her as she stood in her white undergarments, the
cloth short-sleeved and cropped at the calf. She stood staring for
a moment out the window before William touched the back of
her neck and she finished her work.

She removed all, placing her stockings and shoes and under-
finery in the box with the dress, standing naked on the bound-

ary between what had robed her here and the garments William handed her now from the satchel. Her riding clothes. Her gloves and hat.

When she turned to Black Kettle, he kissed her and placed his hand on her chest. "You are of me," he said, "and I am of you."

In the field outside the house William and Evelynne mounted and rode east into the valley of the Great Divide. They made camp partway up the mountain, where they slept among boulders larger than houses. Her America was made of words and the music of words and below the words the silence of rock and mountains and sky. She was not afraid of the Great Unknown. No, she thought, she was deathly afraid. Who commands the word, the world? No man, she reckoned. A woman breathed in, a man breathed out. What brought them to each other in the same breath was a mystery known only to God. In the early dark she took William to her before they continued on to the heights of the Divide.

In the half light they rode through reaches of timber and stone over the southern tip of the pass at Ten Mountain House. She wondered at how woman and man became unclothed in darkness, touched, called out to each other across a chasm of loneliness. Along the fringe of a lake they found a throng of butterflies in a span of flower heads between the water and the forest, and as they rode, the butterflies lighted on their arms and shoulders. *Lycaeana phlaeas americana.* She heard the voice of her father. Wings as if dusted with bronze and fire. The species so beloved to him, the wing pattern he cherished. Gossamer but not to be touched. American Copper. A conducting coil come through the mountain chrysalis. The miracle of spring.

Finally she and Black Kettle took the path toward Bozeman and Billings and the Tongue River lands of the Cheyenne. As they entered Beartooth country, a region colder than the Divide, she heard her father's words again, his voice rooted and thickly drawn: *The trees of Montana claim the mountains. Trees crafted by God and stronger than men.* She remembered him seated in his chair, lead-crystal glass in hand. He spoke of lodgepole forests, words falling from his mouth with nearly no resistance. She had loved his voice. Even inebriated, the resonance was deep and sonorous. *Forests need fire.* His lips glistened. *The essential crucible. Male seeds drop to the shade below and rarely grow. Female cones remain in the tops of the trees.* He flourished his free hand. *Coated in resin. Hard, dark gems. They open only under the cataclysm of fires that sweep the mountain entire!* He wiped his mouth with the back of his hand.

She had witnessed such fires.

When the spark flew, the deadfall kindled and the light went forth to set the world ablaze. The crown fires melted the cones, and then the seeds rained down on the land below. When the fire went cold and winter came, they fermented in the dank earth as they drank water and sun. Then the saplings rose and became trees, robing the mountains more thickly than before.

"My father is dead now," she said.

"He goes to live with all his relations," William said.

She removed her gloves and hat, and her body appeared to be hinged with light, her hands and face almost unnaturally white as she reached for the small spheres of firethorn that hung in long bundles near the shoulders of the horse. She cupped the berries and pulled some free so they fell into her hand like hard drops of blood, cool and dusted with snow, fretted by green crowns. She blew on the berries, and the snow scattered. She took William's hand and meted out half the berries to him. She closed his hand over them, and he smiled at her. He was content. We carry death this way, she thought, like a covenant.

They rode on, and for a great while she watched his shoulders in balance to the rhythm of the horse's gait.

The image of her brother, stoic and refined, came to her. Blood is the mother of us all, she thought. She slipped her hand into her pocket. The firethorn spheres were hard and smooth. She had arrived here beyond self-pity, beyond confusion, and nearly beyond even belief. Black Kettle rode a neck ahead of her. He loved her. She cherished him.

She hoped her father had gone to God. Black Kettle paused as her horse came alongside. The mountains spanned the distance at the edge of all. What is mercy? she questioned. William turned to her, and when he reached and held her jaw, she looked closely at him and drew near and kissed his lips.

EVELYNNE AND BLACK KETTLE, 1935

77.

IN THE HALF dark William wandered with his horse along the base of crowned sandstone that lifted from the land and ribbed the hills. Carved of wind and weather, a flat-topped mountain rose directly ahead of him to the north. Atop the plateau, pines pointed to the sundown sky and he rode his horse up a draw, switchbacking through rock and brush until at last he topped the rise and planed onto open ground where the horse walked among the trees. The place of the dead was below him now, more than a mile to the west. There the warriors lay in their elk-bone breastplates on benches of stone, tomahawks and stone hammers crossed at their chests.

As night set in he breathed the cool air and smelled the scent of timothy on the wind. In the moonlight a light snow fell. He would bring his daughter here one day, he thought.

He felt suddenly heavy and broken and irreparable. He looked up, imagining Raymond, his brother among the stars. His blood pulsed in his chest then like the heart of a horse. Taking courage, he watched the sky for a long time. The light of Quillwork Girl and the Seven Brothers was so close that he spoke aloud, *"Neh ah ehseh."* Thank you. His tongue seemed to him a barbed spear, and yet the heaviness spilled from his body. He halted the horse, lifting his arms to the sky, for his father and mother and for their fathers and mothers, for Evelynne and his own daughter, for his sisters and brothers and all who had fallen at Sand Creek and before Sand Creek and for all who'd fallen since, for Raymond and for Bull Killsnight. He reached into the dark for what might have been. For what was yet to be.

Yes, I will bring my daughter here when she grows tall, he thought. When she is young and strong, we will come here and watch the dawn. In the blackness below, the creatures moved and made their way, bear and badger and wolf, deer and antelope and elk. Coyote moved among them, with the memory of bison a dark shawl on the land. In her lifetime, what burdens she faced he would also carry. What enmity she endured would wound him and call from him the peace he gave to the world. Her mother the source of her strength, all his days he would cherish them and name them beloved.

Out far the moon fell over the river. Again he gave thanks. He turned his horse and went back through the trees, riding south down a long draw and across the plain to the house where his wife and the child awaited him.

THE DWELLING WAS small but sturdy, a construction of log and chinking Black Kettle had taken a summer to complete. Near the edge of the reservation on the land that led to the Big Horn range they had one room and four walls. Fist-sized stones skirted the foundation. A window faced west. Inside, the chimney's small cavern lit and heated the house.

In the three years after she left her father she had miscarried once and carried a stillborn child to term. Now, the winter following her father's death, she brought new life. She was thirty-three years old.

William entered and warmed himself at the fire before he went to lie with Evelynne and hold their baby in his arms. He smelled the sweetness of Evelynne's skin. He drew his daughter close and pressed his face to her face. Her small body, sleepy from suckling, lay on his chest. Her lips still held a droplet of milk. He kissed her. Evelynne propped herself on her elbow, watching him as he held their daughter. She leaned over him, her hair covering the baby and brushing his face.

He touched Evelynne's cheekbone.

The horses stood on the lee side of the house. The wind blew snow east to west.

They closed their eyes, drifting, and everything became still, the fire in its bed of embers, the house in its fall toward morning. In the dark Evelynne and Black Kettle and the child slept. The vault of night was bedecked with light, a coronet of stars over fields that sparked with snow. Evelynne dreamed she saw William with their daughter on a high ridge where they watched a golden eagle in its circuit across the sky, claws tucked to fists, wings containing air and light. They stood in the black brightness of dawn. Dark shadow over the earth, the sky almost unbearably gold. The whole of existence sang with enormity and hunger, and when Black Kettle placed his hand in his daughter's hand, the sun broke the horizon.

Their eyes shone like fire.

Acknowledgments

To my grandmothers, Alice and Catherine: dancers, explorers, wellsprings of wisdom. To my grandfathers, Gerald and Herbert: hunters, hands, moonshine makers, horsemen.

To Lafe Haugen, Russell Tall White Man, Cleveland Bemint, Terry Curley, and Blake Walks Nice for brotherhood and basketball, St. Labre and Lame Deer, southeast Montana, Northern Cheyenne. To Sherman Alexie for friendship and for the line, "White men who did not love the sound of their own mothers' names." To Joe Wilkins for friendship and for the line, "Blood is the mother of us all."

To friend and agent Emily Forland, your kindness has often sustained me in the work. To my editor, Greg Michalson, with deepest appreciation for you and your vision.

With gratitude for these sources: *Cheyenne Memories* by John Stands in Timber, with Margot Liberty; *Love Medecine* by Louise Erdrich; *Spider Woman's Granddaughter: Traditional Tales and Contemporary Writing by Native American Women* by Paula Gunn Allen; *The Healing of American Indian/Alaskan Native Men at Midlife*, doctoral dissertation by Clayton Small; *Fools Crow* by James Welch; *Custer Died for Your Sins* by Vine Deloria, Jr.; *Bury My Heart at Wounded Knee* by

Dee Brown; *Sweet Medicine—Volumes 1 and 2* by Peter J. Powell; *Cheyenne Autumn* by Maria Sandoz; *The Fighting Cheyennes* by George Bird Grinnell; *The Big Sky* by A. B. Guthrie; *Montana 1864* by Ken Egan, Jr.; *War of the Copper Kings* by Carl Glasscock; *James J. Hill: Empire Builder of the Northwest* by Michael Malone.

With respect for the Cheyenne leaders with Black Kettle who survived Sand Creek or died there: Elk Society Headsman, Standing in Water; Kit Fox Headsman, Two Thighs; Yellow Shield, leader of the Bowstrings; and Chiefs Yellow Wolf, Warbonnet, Sand Hill, Bear Tongue, Little Robe, Blacktail Eagle, Spotted Crow, Bear Robe, White Antelope, One Eye, and Bear Man.

Thank you to Cheyenne friends, books, and the Cheyenne Language site for pronunciation and clarity. Any mistakes with regard to the Cheyenne language in this book are mine.

I am indebted to the National Endowment for the Arts for honoring an excerpt of this novel with a literature fellowship. I also want to thank the editors of *McSweeney's* and *Fugue* for featuring selected passages of this work.